THE CENTER

A LANCE SPECTOR THRILLER
BOOK 8

SAUL HERZOG

1

Two years before Roth and Laurel bring Lance back in from the cold.

Two years before the events of Book 1.

Lance Spector held open the elevator door with his foot, leaned forward to check there weren't any surprises waiting for him—left, right, left again—then stepped forward.

He was in a corridor—carpeted, moodily lit with accent lighting, empty. He noted the location of the fire escape. He noted the ice machine. The window. He counted twenty-four doors along the length of the hallway—twelve on each side. Twenty-four hotel rooms. Eighteen recessed ceiling lights. Two fire extinguishers. A hose. He marked all of it—marked it like a tailor sizing up a suit for alteration, like a tinker eyeing the teeth of a horse.

The attention was unnecessary, this was a social call, strictly extracurricular, but he couldn't so easily break the habits of a lifetime. He had a long list of such habits. He couldn't walk past a window without calculating the sight lines, without picturing every possible position from which a sniper might set up a scope. He couldn't exit a highway without memorizing the make and model of every trailing car. He couldn't sleep with his back to a door.

He accepted this—his constant analysis of situations, his assessment and reassessment of every position, every relative advantage, every edge and margin and angle—he accepted his reduction of life to its barest, basest facts as a cost of doing business. They were the price he paid for the life he led. Nothing to worry about, he told himself. Nothing obsessive. Nothing that needed to be hashed out with his agency-assigned shrink during one of the sessions they made him sit through. A man's posture, the shape of the bulge in his jacket, the placement of a woman's purse, the angle of a parked car—these weren't just meaningless details. They were the tools of his trade. They were the very job itself. In his world, they were the difference between life and death.

Every encounter in his day, every interaction with another human being, from the barista pouring his coffee in the morning to the bartender pouring his scotch at night, had the potential to be his last. So that was how he lived. In the knowledge that one day, one of them, some sweet-looking girl bringing his drink, some hard-nosed Russian thug stepping out of a car, *someone* would do him in before he ever saw them coming.

If you want to picture Lance Spector, picture the dead-eyed professional poker player at the table. He plays without joy, without emotion. He holds his tongue. He bides his time. He doesn't move first if he doesn't have to. He doesn't make grand gestures. He waits. With the patience of a reptile, he waits. And when the moment comes, even then, he holds back. He conserves his strength. He keeps everything in reserve.

"Forget what you've seen in the movies." That's what Roth told him at the Farm. "Forget what you've read in books."

"What books?"

"Movies, then."

Lance nodded. He'd forgotten what he'd seen in movies long ago. He'd served in the military. Delta Force. That had cured him of any romantic notions he might have had.

It was Roth who taught him that the spy game was, more than anything else, a game of waiting. A game of watching. "Like poker. You don't win with a single hand. You hollow them out. You grind them at the margins. You haggle over every penny, every chip. You nickel-and-dime everything, over and over, little by little, until they bleed out by a thousand cuts they never knew they had."

"Sounds glamorous."

"We don't lop off the head of the monster, Lance. We tried that. You know what happened?"

"It grew a new head."

Roth nodded. He'd had a soft spot for Lance. Even then. He liked the cut of his jib. "It's not the moments of madness, Lance. It's not the moments of sudden, brutal violence that make us lethal."

"That's why I spent four hours this morning in combat training," Lance said.

"It's patience that takes it," Roth said. "The ability to do the simple things, the mind-numbing things, the same repetitive tasks over and over and over more times than the opponent. That's what takes it for us."

That had been years ago. Lance had come a long way. So long, in fact, that he doubted he'd be able to find his way back now if he tried.

Which was what made *this* so difficult. This corridor. This hotel room he was about to enter. This person he was about to see.

"Quit being such a choirboy," Roth had said when Lance first reported it.

"It's an indiscretion."

Roth rolled his eyes. "It's not an indiscretion. It's a lay. Enjoy it, for God's sake. *I* sure would."

"I bet you would."

"No man is an island, Lance. Feel something for once."

"Feel something?" Lance said. "That's dangerous advice."

"It's advice you need to take."

"It's a breach of protocol. She's my handler."

"You think you're the first asset to get in bed with a handler?" Roth said. "It's practically part of the program design, you ninny. Why do you think they're all women? All bombshells, for that matter? That's just a happy coincidence, is it?"

And Roth had a point. They were all bombshells. Not least, Clarice. And as for program design, that wasn't so hard to believe either. The CIA was certainly capable of it. The Special Operations Group was a kill unit. It cleaned up problems so that the government and the military didn't have to. It got its hands dirty. Against that, a little workplace sexual exploitation was small potatoes. "So you're not going to do anything about it?" Lance said.

"Do anything? What do you want? A fluffer?"

That had been a few months ago, and try as he might, Lance still had to admit he'd liked things better the old way. Before he and Clarice were an item. Before they'd gone and complicated everything with emotions and feelings and *connection*. There'd been less room for misunderstanding then. Everyone had known where they stood.

Not that he had any cause for complaint. Clarice was the full package, a *grade-A* you-know-what with an engine under the hood that was tuned like a fighter jet. She had kick that would put a stallion to shame. She certainly could have had a lineup of suitors at Langley if she'd wanted. Hell, she could have hosted auditions.

But no. She chose Lance. More than ten years her senior, which might as well have been a million if the music she listened to was anything to go by. Lance was a man of simple tastes. He liked Pearl Jam. He liked Coltrane. He liked John Lee Hooker. What Clarice listened to, he didn't know what that was.

He was still in his thirties, but that made him a dinosaur in her world. They might as well have been from different planets. But that hadn't stopped her from pulling him into the janitor's closet at work one day and, not twenty feet from Levi Roth's desk, doing things to him that would have made a dead man rise out of his grave. Best sixty seconds Lance had ever spent, that was for sure. She could have tried out for the US Olympics gymnastics team if she'd wanted.

But despite all that—the fireworks in the bedroom, the lingerie that would have made a stripper blush, the positions that looked like they'd been taken straight from the pages of the *Kama Sutra*—he still liked things better the old way.

He couldn't help it. It was what it was. The problem, well, one problem, was that he still thought of her first and foremost as his handler. That was her primary function, her *raison d'etre,* the reason she was allowed into his life in the first place. Even in the heat of the moment—the height of passion, as they called it—when they were looking into each others' eyes at the very moment of ecstasy, he looked at her and saw a professional auxiliary. A tool that made him more effective, more lethal, in the field. His handler.

Never had he told her he loved her. Never had he thought of her as a girlfriend. Never had he imagined a future with her beyond what they already had.

This, whatever *this* was, was a sideshow. It was onion rings. The work they did for Roth was the steak.

And the funny thing was, despite all her hard work—and *work* was the operative word—he had the distinct impression she felt exactly the same way. For all the outpourings of emotion, the romantic gestures, for all her efforts to create meaning and intimacy between them, all his misgivings about the relationship seemed to be completely mutual. She didn't love him. She wasn't under his spell. She was just *trying* to be in love with him.

In her apartment once, he'd found a book in the drawer next to her bed—the drawer, mind, not out in the open—called *How to Fall in Love with Anyone.* One of the techniques it recommended was to stare into someone's eyes for four minutes without speaking or looking away. He knew for a fact she'd tried it on him. He remembered her doing it. She'd kept telling him not to talk. Many of the supposedly deep conversations they'd had too —her sharing of childhood memories, her confessions of secret desires, and fears, and regrets—were also in the book. There was sexual chemistry between them, that much was undeniable, but the way she was built, she would have had sexual chemistry with a mannequin.

In fact, increasingly, he had the feeling that the only reason one of them hadn't ended the whole thing long ago was that it afforded another type of benefit. It proved—and not just to the shrinks, but to themselves too, and anyone else on the sixth floor who worried about such things—that they were still sane, still healthy, still capable of empathy and emotional attachment. The CIA worried about such things. The Group certainly did. Guys went off the deep end when they lost too much of themselves. This was a green check mark on both of their psych evaluations.

Lance almost found it easier to think of the relationship entirely in those terms, as if it was purely an aspect of his psych eval, not so different from the therapy sessions they made him undertake whenever he got back from a kill.

Maybe that really was all it was. What had Roth called it? *Program design*?

Or worse, had Roth simply ordered Clarice to seduce him? Had she been following orders all along? Was this all an act, a means of keeping a valuable but temperamental piece of machinery effective in the field for longer?

There was an unsettling thought—an order from Roth's desk—it was a little too much like having a third participant in the bed. Lance felt an involuntary shiver run down his spine. Was that what was going on? Had Roth put her up to the whole thing? Or was that just more of his paranoia talking?

He pushed the thought from his mind as he walked along the corridor. He was there to rest, to recuperate, not re-evaluate his entire personal life through the prism of yet another potential conspiracy. Clarice wasn't a threat. She was a girlfriend. *Enjoy it for what it is*, he told himself. *It will all be gone soon enough if past experience is anything to go by.*

He looked out the window as he passed it—imagining sightlines and sniper positions—and decided to just trust her. It was a beautiful evening, the setting sun casting oblique rays of light through the city skyline like the outstretched fingers of a deity. *Believe in something,* he told himself. *Believe.*

And believe he did, or tried to.

He was on the thirty-eighth floor of the Manhattan Four Seasons, located midway between Park Avenue and Madison. The hotel had been her idea, of course—he'd have been just as comfortable at the EconoLodge back in Deweyville—but she'd been insistent.

"We need this," she'd said over the cafeteria table at Langley a few days earlier. "*You* need it."

"I need silk sheets and a minibar that charges sixteen dollars for a tiny packet of cashew nuts?"

"Oh, you're familiar with the minibar offerings, are you?"

He was, actually—that exact hotel was charged

to more GRU and FSB expense accounts than any other hotel in the country. He said, "I know every detail of the place, down to the brand of shampoo they use in the bathrooms and the secret entrance on 57th Street for their four-grand-a-night hookers."

"I see," she'd said, clenching her jaw the way she had a habit of.

He'd never noticed that when she was just his handler—the tension at her temples, the narrowing of the eyes. Now, he felt like it was the only expression he ever got from her. Nothing he said was ever quite right, and the hooker reference had been thrown in half on purpose just to get a rise from her. "I don't even know how you came up with the idea," he'd added. "Roth's got a perfectly nice fishing cabin on—"

"Here!" she'd said, flinging her copy of *Vogue* magazine in his face. It landed in his plate, splashing gravy onto his white shirt.

She shrugged defiantly.

He took the magazine out of his lunch and looked at a *Buzzfeed*-style article entitled:

> Seven ultra-high-end NYC hotel rooms guaranteed to rekindle your fizzling love life.

"I see," he'd said, taking a sip of coffee and

putting the magazine down deliberately on the table.

"What's wrong?" she said, knowing full well what it was.

He drank more coffee and said, "*Fizzling*?"

"Oh, come on," she said. "You're being petty. I didn't mean it that way at all."

She had, though. She'd meant it exactly *that way* and had, in fact, flung it *that way* in his face, right into his beef stroganoff.

He'd booked the room there and then, a weekend in New York at eleven hundred dollars a night with restaurant reservations to match, as well as tickets to a modern ballet production that he imagined even a Juilliard professor would have had a hard time sitting through.

He had it all to look forward to now, he thought—two days and two nights of luxury and romance that he was dreading more than a visit to a Lubyanka interrogation room. He wasn't sure how much it would help with the *fizzle*, but there it was.

Clarice was supposed to already be in the room, but when he knocked on the door, there was no answer. He knocked again, glancing at his watch. He checked his phone. Sure enough, there was a voice message. It had come in fifteen minutes earlier without his noticing. He pressed play.

Sorry, babe. Running an errand. There's a key for you with the concierge.

He made his way back to the lobby, then back up to the thirty-eighth floor and let himself in.

It was nice—he couldn't deny that—understated luxury with a view across the park that was like something out of a Woody Allen film. Was it worth two car payments a night? He wasn't sure. But then, what did he know? He was a dinosaur. This was what people did now.

He put down his bag and placed a coffee capsule in the fancy machine, an ethical Rwandan blend if the label was to be believed, and waited for it to brew. When it was done, he brought the tiny porcelain cup over to the bed and kicked off his shoes. Clarice had left a few clues of her presence scattered around the room—a phone charger on the nightstand, a smart leather suitcase under the window, a black negligee on the floor next to it. Lance eyed the negligee like he would a feral animal. In the reflection of a mirror, he could see into the bathroom. She'd taken a shower. He counted four full-sized towels on the floor, as if she'd decided to make a point of getting her money's worth from the laundry service.

He looked at his watch, wondering how long she was going to be. It was a quarter to seven—thirty minutes since she'd left the message and an hour and fifteen until their reservation at the Michelin-starred *Le Jardinier*, which, according to the same *Vogue* article, combined flavors and techniques from East and West to create a 'veritable culinary wonderland.'

He thought about calling her, though he knew she wouldn't pick up. The only thing that would have caused her to interrupt this special weekend was work—she took it as seriously as he did—and that meant she'd call when she could. It was normal enough. They were used to it. Secrets were their bread and butter. Even as asset and handler, they had their secrets. They'd accepted it long ago. He thought about taking a shower, but just as he got up from the bed, the electronic lock on the door clicked.

The door swung open, and in walked Clarice, marching toward him, a loaded Beretta 92 pistol pointed right at his chest.

2

An elegant woman in her early sixties, dressed in sensible three-inch heels and a tailored tweed jacket, strode purposefully across the sixth-floor office of the CIA's New Headquarters building at Langley holding aloft a yellow envelope. Levi Roth watched her approach through the glass wall of the conference room and slowly rose to his feet. "It's arrived, then?" he said.

His chief of staff, Clementine Pye, shut the door behind her and approached the desk. She put the envelope in his hand and said, in a British accent that might have been perfected in Buckingham Palace itself, "You're not going to like this one bit."

"Oh?" he said, looking at the innocuous-looking envelope.

She mouthed the next word rather than voicing it aloud, as if its very utterance were something indecent. "Rat."

"You're sure?" Roth said quietly.

"Look inside."

He turned the envelope over and examined both sides, front and back, as if the blank paper might tell him something.

"You're procrastinating," she said.

The envelope had already been unsealed—indeed, it had been tested for every explosive, pathogen, toxin, and electronic bug known to the scientists in the CIA lab—and been given the all-clear. Roth unfolded the flap carefully and tapped the envelope against the surface of the desk, coaxing from it a six-by-eight-inch black and white photograph printed on a matte, almost velvet-textured paper.

"According to the lab," Clementine said, "that's a baryta-based 290-gram Unibrom photographic paper."

"Is that supposed to mean something to me?" Roth said, picking it up carefully.

"No," she said, "but they thought you'd be interested to know it's produced and marketed by a company named Slavich, based in Yaroslavl Oblast. It's sold only in Russia."

Roth looked closely at the picture—a man stepping out of a yellow New York taxicab—and guessed from the angle that it had been taken from across the street. Apart from the man's face—which was clear enough, though he was wearing sunglasses—there wasn't much to it.

"Hmm," he said noncommittally, unable to see

why it had created such a flurry of excitement when it came in.

"The delivery instruction specified you by name," Clementine said.

Roth nodded. That wasn't good—his name and job title weren't exactly listed on the CIA's 'Contact Us' page—but it wasn't enough to prove they'd been infiltrated. Certainly, it wasn't enough to conclude they had a rat.

"The cab's identifiable from the medallion number," Clementine continued, pointing to a partially visible sign on the cab's roof. "We're tracking down the company to see if there's anything else they can tell us, but we do think we know the location of the drop-off already."

"From this?" Roth said, looking at the grainy, out-of-focus background in the picture. As near as he could tell, it showed nothing more than the side of a building.

"That wall is classic Carrère and Hastings limestone," Clementine said.

"Carrère and Hastings?"

"An architecture firm from New York's *Beaux Arts* period. Those lines at the corner of the wall are a very distinctive rustication detail."

"Indeed," Roth said. "*Beaux Arts*," he added slightly skeptically.

"The guys in the lab say the building is the Russian Consulate-General on East 91st Street. Just off Central Park."

"All that from this?"

She shrugged. "They seemed confident."

"I'm sure they did."

"The man's GRU," she continued, ignoring his tone—a skill she was well-practiced at. "Flew into JFK on a commercial flight from Moscow yesterday. We suspect he's a direct report to the top floor."

"Does he have a name?"

"Daniil Grechko."

"And it definitely wasn't one of our guys who took this photo?"

"Definitely not. We weren't even monitoring the building. We had no reason to."

"And I suppose we didn't flag Daniil Grechko when he landed either?"

"We did not. He used false papers. We missed him."

Roth looked intently at the photo again and said, "Forgive me if this seems obtuse, but doesn't this rather suggest they're the ones with a rat in the house? I mean, whoever sent this photo is trying to help us. They wanted us to know Grechko was in the country."

She got that look then, that guileful smile she always had before she made a big revelation, and said, "You haven't looked at the back yet."

He turned over the photo, knowing it could only bear bad news. And it did. He pursed his lips as he read the words someone had scrawled on it with a blue ballpoint pen. It was a list. Four items. In a simpler world, it might have been the shopping list of a classic car collector, but Roth did not live in a simpler world.

Mustang
Rebel
Camaro
Hornet

His pulse quickened, though he did his best not to show it. "So," he said, clearing his throat, which had suddenly gone dry, "this is what got it up the chain so quickly?"

"It set off a few alarms, yes."

"One or two," Roth said, his heart still thumping in his chest as if he'd just run up two flights of stairs. "And we have no idea who it's from?"

"A DHL courier dropped it off at the Federal Building on H Street a couple of hours ago."

"But no idea who sent it?"

She shook her head. "The courier picked it up at a DHL drop-off location in Alexandria. CCTV of the location shows a man in a motorcycle helmet dropping something off at about the right time, but we haven't been able to identify him."

"Did he pay for delivery?"

"Cash."

Roth caught her eye, then looked away. This was bad. They both knew it. Those four words summed up an entire operation, the entire Special

Operations Group—it represented years of planning and countless painful sacrifices. It represented Roth's life's work. He sat down heavily on his seat and looked again at the back of the photo. All four codenames. "If they have these," he said, "there's no telling what they have."

"They could have the asset's real names," Clementine said. "They could have *my* name, for God's sake. They could have the combination to your locker at the country club."

"Let's not lose our heads, Clem."

She didn't smile.

There was a minibar in the corner of the room, and Roth glanced at it. He could have used a stiff scotch but knew she wouldn't join him if he offered. He chewed his lip, thinking, and Clementine remained where she was, standing in front of his desk like an orderly waiting to be dismissed. "Tell me there isn't anything else," he said, unable to conceal the dread in his voice.

"That's about the size of it, for now."

"For now," he said, looking at his watch. It was after eight. "You'll be wanting to get home to that husband of yours."

"I'm not going anywhere," she said. "Not tonight. The old sod can put something in the microwave."

She wasn't one to jump ship in a crisis. Roth appreciated that. "The assets are definitely at risk," he said. "Their asses are right in the wind."

"And we can't loop in the handlers..." Clementine started before letting the words trail off without finishing the sentence.

"Because we don't know if one of them's our rat," Roth said, finishing the thought for her. He threw the photo onto the desk and said, "Well, you were right, as usual."

"You'll have to be a little more specific," she said wryly.

He smiled. "When you said I wasn't going to like it."

"Ah," she said. "Well, it's not good, is it?"

"You always did have a knack for understatement, Clementine."

They were both quiet then. Roth got up and went to the wall of glass that separated the conference room from the rest of the office. The Special Operations Group occupied the entire sixth floor of the building and was supposed to be the tightest of tight ships, the topmost of top secrets, the riddle wrapped inside the mystery wrapped inside the enigma. It had been designed from the ground up to avoid precisely this type of infiltration. This shouldn't have been happening. But here they were.

He looked out at the desks of the specialists and handlers he'd handpicked and thought of the background checks he'd personally conducted, his prying examination of every detail, every secret, of their personal lives. He'd interviewed them for hours using CIA interrogation tactics that were more commonly reserved for the enemy. He'd surprised them with unannounced visits to their homes, to their family members' homes. He'd tracked down old lovers, old enemies, old neighbors, doctors, teachers, friends, business associates. He knew them better than they knew themselves, and now, with a chill, he realized that one of them had betrayed him. Had betrayed all of them. They had a rat in the house, a stranger in the bed, and it was not a nice feeling.

Apart from himself and Clementine, the Group consisted of only four handlers, each independently responsible for one of four assets. In addition, there was a team of twenty-seven specialists who provided operational support. He flicked a switch on the wall, and the glass turned instantly opaque. Then he faced Clementine and said quietly, "If we don't fix this, we'll have to scorch the earth. Burn it all down. Liquidate everything."

She said nothing, but her jaw was set as firmly as a vise. He knew she understood him. They were both silent for what felt like a very long time, and then she said, "Let's not jump to any conclusions, Levi. There are steps that can be taken."

"Steps," Roth repeated. He was all too aware of the *steps* that were available to him. They weren't pretty. Blood would be spilled. People would suffer. Innocent people. *His* people.

"You just need to decide who you can still trust," she said.

He crossed the room. The sixth floor was prime real estate. He'd had to defend his claim to it against multiple other department heads, including the director. In the end, it was his relationship with the president that clinched it. The view from the window overlooked a wide bend of the Potomac and a length of the George Washington Memorial Parkway that stretched along its west bank. He looked out at the moon's reflection on the river, making it a silver ribbon. A thin line of red and white lights twinkled on the parkway. Traffic was light. He focused on the view to avoid having to look at Clementine.

"Present company included," she added, and he could hear the discomfort in her voice.

The sixth floor, *the Group*, as they called it—he, Clementine, the handlers, the assets, and the specialists—formed a tight-knit group of thirty-seven people. Ruling out himself, and himself alone, that left thirty-six suspects. No one was automatically excused. Not even her. They both knew it, both understood the reasons for it, but that didn't make it any more palatable.

The assets—officially paramilitary operatives—were secretly acknowledged to be the most elite human units in the nation's arsenal. Recruited exclusively from Navy's SEAL Team Six, Air Force's 24th Special Tactics Squadron, Marine Corps' MARSOC, and Army's Delta Force, they were the true tip of the spear. They were the president's *tertio optio,* his third option, for those situations where neither of the other two—diplomacy and all-out military force—sufficed.

Officially, none of them existed—not the assets, not the handlers and specialists, not even Roth and Clementine standing there in their top-floor office. There would be no stars for any of them on the Agency's memorial wall when they died. There would be no honor guards and draped flags and military trumpeters at their funerals. There would be no funerals at all, in fact. By classified executive order, Roth was required to maintain such extreme secrecy that—should it ever prove necessary—he was authorized to order the liquidation of his own team. Entirely.

That was what made this moment so fraught. So *distasteful.* It wasn't just the rat's head that was on the block. It was everyone's.

Everyone on the team knew this, of course. They knew what they'd signed up for. If their existence ever became a problem, a liability to the White House or the Pentagon, then it would be Roth, and not the enemy, who came for them in the night. It was just a fact of their existence, never spoken, never dwelled upon, but always there, under the surface, eating away at all of them.

"You know who I trust," Roth said at last. It wasn't a question, and he spoke hesitantly, uncertain still where all of this was going to take them. He turned toward her and was surprised by the look on her face, the color on her cheeks. She was embarrassed.

"I didn't want to presume," she said awkwardly. It was almost girlish the way she said it.

Not for the first time, he wondered how things might have turned out between them if circumstances had been different. Pushing that thought from his mind, he said, “The way I see it, this is a coin with two sides.”

“Like so many coins,” she said coyly.

He smiled. It was times like this that he appreciated her wit most. “We may have a rat,” he said, “but so do they. And we both know how to go about catching rats.”

Clementine nodded. “With bait,” she said.

3

Lance woke with a start. His phone was vibrating on the nightstand, and he picked it up.

"What is it?" Clarice mumbled from across the bed, her voice still groggy from sleep and the copious amount of wine she'd had with dinner.

The pistol had been a joke. She'd followed it up with a pair of handcuffs, then the pyrotechnics and physical contortions that made her such a champion in Lance's eyes, at least in the bedroom. They'd been late for their dinner reservation, of course, which the *maitre d'* hadn't been forgiving of. "Your table," he'd said, pronouncing it the French way, as if the 'e' wasn't there, "your *tabl, monsieur*, is no more."

"Kaput, is it?"

"*Oui, monsieur.*" A flourish of a gloved hand. "Kaput."

A hundred-dollar bill remedied that, which had been money well spent, in Lance's opinion.

"It's Roth," he said, looking at his phone. "I have to check in."

"He knows we're in New York," she said irritably. "I reminded him before I left."

Lance hauled himself out of the bed and switched on the lamp. Clarice turned her back to him dramatically, shifting as far to the other side of the bed as she could without falling off. She was annoyed. Work calls had not been part of the *Vogue* article's prescription for rekindling romance.

"There's no point getting upset," he said. "It could just as easily have been you he called."

"Sure," she said, but she wasn't placated.

Lance shrugged. Truth be told, he wasn't all that bothered by being called in. If anything, he was relieved. He'd been sleeping terribly—the *Le Jardinier* chef had put out an extravagant multi-course tasting menu, complete with handpicked wine pairings—and Lance's dreams had been extremely unsettled. *Culinary wonderlands*, it seemed, were another of life's finer things he wasn't cut out for.

The ballet had been even worse. He'd tried his absolute utmost to be a good sport—Clarice had been watching him as closely as any interrogator ever had—and he'd laughed, cried, and applauded at all the right moments. Or so he'd thought. The whole thing had been an hours-long test of his endurance, of his ability to grin and bear it while completely concealing the fact he was in pain. He'd been trained in the art, but it seemed last night he'd failed. He wasn't sure what moment had been his undoing, but by the time they got back to the hotel, Clarice had stopped talking to him.

"Don't even bother," she'd said when he'd held up the black negligee from her suitcase. He'd been relieved. He'd never been the type of fighter to go for a second round.

He grabbed his phone and brought it into the bathroom, where he sat on the can with his shorts pulled up and dialed the security codes required to reach Roth.

"Please wait," an automated voice said. It was followed by a series of analog clicks and beeps before Levi Roth's gravelly baritone filled the line. "Lance? You still in New York?"

"Yes, with Clarice, and your timing's not exactly—"

"Tell her I'm sorry, but her plans for the weekend are shot. You're going to be out of the country for the next forty-eight hours, at least. I'll make it up to her."

"Oh, you will?"

"Not like that."

"Be my guest."

"You should have been a comedian. We're wasting you here."

"It's me you'll have to make it up to," Lance said. "I'm the one who's going to be in the dog house."

"In any case," Roth said, "be downstairs in ten. I've got a car waiting to take you to Teterboro."

"A car? How chivalrous."

"You know me," Roth said. "Ten minutes." He hung up, and the line went dead so abruptly that Lance had to check that the call hadn't been dropped. It hadn't.

He stood and looked at the reflection staring back at him in the mirror. His face was tired—*weathered* was the word, he hoped. He took a very quick shower, then went back to the bedroom with a towel around his waist and a toothbrush in his mouth.

Clarice was sitting on the bed, looking at him like a puppy being left at a pound in January, and he wiped toothpaste from his mouth with the back of his hand and said, "That was Roth."

"No kidding."

"He wants me to take a cab out to Teterboro."

"Did he say where you were going?"

Lance ignored the question. She was his handler, but if Roth wanted her to know where he was going, he'd send her the file soon enough. "I'll be gone two days," he said. "That means the hotel's—"

"A bust," she said sullenly.

"I'm sorry," he said, spreading his hands as if to show his powerlessness. As he did, the towel fell to the ground.

She said, "Looks like you're more excited about going to work than you were about me last night."

He looked down, then back up. Nothing witty came to mind, so he didn't say anything.

She rolled her eyes, then got up from the bed and put a capsule in the coffee machine, slamming it shut with more force than was necessary. He finished getting dressed, and she handed him the coffee she'd made.

"I really am sorry," he said, taking a sip. "I was looking forward to—"

"No, you weren't."

He looked at her, wondering how much longer the two of them were going to keep up the charade, then gathered up his things. She helped, handing him his coat like a dutiful wife seeing him off to work. If she didn't end things soon, he would have to. It wasn't right to keep her tied up like this, wasting her time. She deserved to be with someone who appreciated her.

"All right," he said, giving her a kiss—a platonic peck on the cheek—before squeezing by her awkwardly to get to the door.

"Stay safe," she said.

He looked back and gave her a curt nod, then shut the door on what had to have been one of the least successful romantic getaways room 3819 of the Midtown Four Seasons had seen in quite a while.

He made his way down the corridor quickly and called the elevator. While waiting for it, he thought he heard a noise from their room. "Clarice?"

There was no answer.

4

Clarice watched Lance leave—he gave the distinct impression he couldn't get out of the room fast enough—then hurried to the door and watched him through the peephole. She could see as far as the elevator, where he stood waiting. Her purse was on a side table, and she reached for it while keeping an eye pressed to the door. The bag slipped and fell, its metal chain clanging noisily.

She froze, her heart pounding.

Out in the corridor, Lance looked up. He said something, her name maybe, and it looked for a second like he was going to come back. Then, the elevator dinged. He took a last look in her direction, then stepped in and disappeared. She let out a sigh of relief, then picked up the purse and rummaged through it for her phone.

Her first call was to Langley, where she told a specialist to get her a list of every flight in and out of Teterboro that morning. Then she checked the peephole again—half caution, half paranoia—and found herself putting the chain on the door just in case. She checked her messages—the specialist still hadn't sent the list—and made herself one of the capsule coffees while she waited. She brought it to the bed and sipped it until she felt her phone vibrate.

The list from the specialist contained over sixty flights, mostly East Coast traffic but a few longer-haul shots to Mexico, the West Coast, and the Caribbean. Three flights were transatlantic, a Gulfstream G-IV to London Gatwick, a Challenger 604 to Marseilles, and a longer-range Falcon 7X to Domodedovo Airport south of Moscow. She'd have bet dollars to donuts Lance was on that Falcon and considered having its tail number cross-referenced against a list of CIA-owned jets. She didn't, though. Too much digging would attract attention. It would look like she was worried about something, hiding something.

Instead, she fired off an encrypted message to her handler.

Mustang possibly inbound to Moscow.

It usually took him hours to reply, but an assassin flying to Moscow was precisely the type of thing to grab his attention. She nodded knowingly when the three dots of a response being typed appeared instantly.

Who's the target?

She had no idea who the target was. She didn't even know for sure there was a target, or indeed, if Lance was headed to Moscow at all, but that was no way to play her hand. Her value to them depended entirely on her access to information. The more she had, the more they liked her. It was as simple as that. *Quid pro quo.* If she had nothing, she became nothing.

The understanding, of course, was that none of it would ever be used in a way that could be traced back to her. It was to be treated like Winston Churchill's *Ultra*, only being used if there was an ironclad alternate explanation for how it was obtained.

"A dead mole's good to no one," was what the handler had said. That had been during the honeymoon phase—the period of her recruitment—when he'd been full of promises and assurances and would have said anything to get in her good graces. "There's no opulence like Moscow opulence," he'd said, his face close enough to hers she could smell the vodka on his breath. "The luxury is, how you say, *unbridled*, yes?"

"*Unbridled*?" she'd said skeptically. "That's quite... *something*."

"Whatever you like, you can have," he'd continued, failing to register her skepticism. "Nice things. Naughty things. Even bad things, Clarice. Terrible things. *Nasty*." His eyebrow rose when he said the last word, like it had some specific meaning between them.

"I assure you," she'd said, "I have no need of anything *nasty*."

He gave her that look again, like there could be no secrets between them, and said, "Don't doubt me, Clarice. This is real. If there's something you want, anything, no matter how...."

"*Nasty?*"

He laughed. "The oligarchs are the richest men on earth. They own our country. The largest on earth. They don't just rule it. They *own* it. An empire that traverses eleven timezones, that's half the world."

"*Almost* half the world."

"Eleven twenty-fourths, then, if you're a stickler."

"I am a stickler."

"They are kings in the truest sense," he'd continued, growing more animated as his claims grew. "They are emperors. When their favor shines on you, there's no feeling in the world like it. It's intoxicating, Clarice. It's ecstasy."

Ecstasy. What girl didn't need a little of that in

her life? "You like to make promises, Mr Grechko." That was his name, or the one he'd given her, at least. Daniil Grechko. A little digging later confirmed him as a top-floor operator in the Prime Directorate. She still hadn't figured out who precisely he answered to, though he was certainly high up enough that his promises held water. When he said he could pay, he meant it. Of course, it also meant his bark had bite. She didn't want to get on the wrong side of that.

"Promises?" he'd said. "Clarice, this is just the beginning. How long do you think the Aquarium's been trying to get inside Roth's panties?"

The Aquarium was how the Russians referred to the massive concrete edifice that housed GRU headquarters. They took pride in how monstrously large it was, as if the number of rooms it had dictated its power. Grechko himself had mentioned that its construction used more concrete than the 1980 Moscow Olympic Stadium.

"Roth's panties?" Clarice said.

"How long have they been trying to spread his legs?" he said, raising a hand and spreading two fingers in a V. "Spread his legs and give him a thorough fucking?" He licked the air between his fingers.

She looked away.

"Thirty years!" he announced with a slap on the bar, spittle flying from his mouth and landing on her lip.

She wiped it away.

"Thirty years!" he said again. "A lifetime, they've

waited to slit his whore throat and skewer him like a squealing pig."

"I see," Clarice said calmly, wishing he'd quieten down.

"I think you do see," he said slyly. "I think you see very well. You know they'll pay too, don't you, you little minx?"

"I wouldn't presume—"

He put a hand on her leg then—just above the knee—and gave it a little squeeze. She pushed it away instantly, though she wasn't as scandalized as all that. She'd chosen the skirt especially—a prim, gray herringbone, like a British schoolgirl. She'd yet to meet a superior who didn't approve.

"You're not as innocent as you let on, are you, Clarice Snow?"

"Careful, Daniil. I haven't agreed to anything yet."

"Oh, come now. You agreed the moment you set foot in this bar. Just showing your face sealed your fate. There's no going back now."

"Then why are you still trying to sell me?"

He smiled. It was a thin, mean smile, and there was a hunger in it. His hand moved again to her thigh, and her eyes followed it like a lizard watching a fly.

"You never declared this meeting, did you?" he said. "You never told anyone on your side you'd been approached."

"Maybe I still will."

He shook his head, and his hand moved an inch

farther up her thigh. "The die is cast," he said. "You've made your bed."

She shrugged, as if there was still some doubt in the matter, as if it could still go either way, and leaned away from him, recrossing her legs.

His hand withdrew, but the mean little grin remained. "You're too smart a girl for make-believe. We're in bed together now, you and I. For better or worse."

She said nothing, but they both knew he was right. She'd sealed her fate the moment she showed up. She was already a traitor. That was the whole point of meeting face-to-face. To put her fate in his hands.

She looked around the bar, a busy Midtown place for the after-work crowd. She saw nothing out of the ordinary, all suits and white blouses and nine-ounce Chardonnays, but she had no doubt there was a camera somewhere. She was being filmed. She'd given them their *Kompromat*, the only currency they understood, the only guarantee they accepted.

"Now that we're on the same page," Grechko said, "I suppose I should ask your motivations,

"For defecting? Please tell me you're not looking for a true believer."

"A true believer! Hah!" He slapped the bar again. "We stopped looking for those a very long time ago."

"I have no doubt."

"But in my experience, Clarice, it's never *just* the money that leads someone to a decision like this."

"Well, there's a first time for everything."

He shook his head. "An interesting girl like you, so mysterious, so multifaceted? I don't believe for a second you're here for the money."

She shrugged. "Believe whatever you want. It doesn't matter what I tell you, in any case. Your people will have compiled a hundred-page file on me already. That's what the top floor will believe, regardless of what I say here."

He looked at her closely, as if reading her thoughts, as if sizing up all the countless variables that had brought a nice girl like her to a place like this, and said, "I suppose they will."

"But not you?"

"Well, Clarice, you see, I've had the pleasure of reading that file. And, first off, let me tell you, it's a lot longer than a hundred pages. A *lot* longer."

"And it made for interesting reading?"

"Interesting would be an understatement...."

"I'm sensing a *but*."

"Well, it was," he shrugged, "*incomplete.*"

Clarice thought about that, about what might be in the file, then forced her mind back to the present, the bustling bar, the here and now. "I'll tell you this much, Mr Grechko, since you're interested. The one thing you can trust me to do is act in my own interest."

He kept looking at her, squinting his eyes, scanning for tells—seeing her the way his decades in the hive of the Russian intelligence apparatus had trained him to see things. For the life of her, she wished he'd stop. She'd have preferred a hand on the knee to that piercing gaze. "Some would say you've already disproved that just by coming here," he said.

"Disproved what?"

"That you act in your own interest. Just by being here, doing what you're doing, unless I'm missing something, some would say either you're lying or a madwoman."

"And which would you say?"

His squinty eyes kept her fixed—a second passed, then five—and the air grew heavy between them. After what felt like a very long time, he leaned back in his seat and relieved the tension. He waved a hand in front of his face like he was swatting a fly. "In my experience, these things usually boil down to daddy issues."

Her face flushed, and she tried to hide it.

He smiled. "Touched a nerve?"

"That would suit you perfectly, wouldn't it?"

He nodded, though his face remained blank. "The money's nice too, I suppose."

"Not just money. *Unbridled* money. *Unbridled* luxury."

"You're mocking me."

"I would never."

"You are," he said, "but it doesn't matter, so long as you know what you want, however *nasty*."

"I don't know why you keep saying that."

"Don't pretend you don't know what I mean."

"I have no idea."

"Come, Clarice. We all have our naughty desires. It's the bad things that get our blood flowing, don't you think? The *nasty* things. And it's the *really* nasty things that get a girl like you to do a thing like this."

5

Lance stepped out of the elevator, empty but for a snoozing guard at the concierge's desk, and walked briskly through the lobby. The guard was drooling a little, and the top few buttons of his shirt were open. He roused himself with a snort as Lance walked by. "Car, sir?" he said, fumbling with his collar.

"As you were, soldier," Lance said, pushing the rotating lobby doors and exiting onto 57th Street. What he'd expected was a waiting cab. What he found was Levi Roth's enormous custom Cadillac Escalade, complete with bombproof undercarriage, bulletproof tinted windows, and a specially built Hemi V8 engine. Strange, he thought. Why the smoke and mirrors? And Langley was a four-hour drive away at the best of times. Something very serious must have gone wrong for Roth to cut into his beauty sleep and make that trip.

Lance descended the steps to the car and

opened the door. Roth was sitting in the back with an early edition of *The Times* on his lap, open to the crossword.

"What's going on?" Lance said, holding the door like he suddenly wasn't sure he wanted to get in.

"Good morning to you, too," Roth said, taking his pen from his mouth and tapping it on his lip.

"No, seriously," Lance said. "What are you doing here?"

"Get in," Roth said, making room for him on the seat.

Roth's usual driver was up front, his black cap tilted in front of his eyes like a baseball pitcher's. For reasons Lance had yet to decipher, Roth always had his drivers wear an old-style chauffeur's uniform. It gave meetings in the back of his car a strange air of formality.

"Something's happened," Lance said. "You wouldn't be here if it wasn't serious."

"Get in," Roth said again, returning his attention to the crossword as if the situation were the most ordinary thing in the world.

Lance climbed in and said, "Harry," by way of acknowledgment to the driver.

"Lance," the driver said with a nod, then raised the glass privacy screen that separated him from the passenger compartment.

The car pulled away slowly from the hotel, and Roth continued puzzling over his newspaper. Lance waited for him to say something, glancing around at whatever clues there were to take in. There weren't many. Roth was dressed impeccably, as usual, in a navy cashmere suit and light blue shirt. Propped next to him on the seat was a thin leather briefcase. Lance cleared his throat, but Roth still refused to look up from the crossword. "I'm sorry," Lance said. "Do you need a hand with that?"

"Hypothetical situations," Roth said. "Three letters."

"Ifs," Lance said.

Roth nodded and scrawled in the answer while Lance looked out the back window, taking note of the license plates of any vehicles behind them. "We're not going to Teterboro, are we?" he said.

"We are not," Roth said, still refusing to quit the crossword. The man had an innate sense of the dramatic. He could never resist holding onto whatever scrap of a secret a situation gave him.

"You didn't want Clarice to know about this," Lance said.

"I don't want anyone to know," Roth said. "The circle is you, me, Kathleen, and the driver. Understood?"

Lance nodded.

"I wouldn't have looped you in either if I didn't have to."

Lance said nothing. He'd been in the game long enough to know something serious had happened. Something out of the ordinary. To go around his handler, to be here like this in person, it wasn't Roth's usual MO. It didn't bode well. He leaned back in his seat and waited.

At length, Roth folded up the newspaper and slapped it down deliberately on the seat between them. "I'm not going to lie," he said, turning to Lance. "It's nothing good."

"When is it ever?" Lance said.

Roth pulled the briefcase flat onto his lap and snapped the two clasps on the side. The lid swung open to reveal a single black-and-white photograph.

"What's this?" Lance said, eyeing the photo.

"It arrived yesterday, addressed to me personally."

"By name?"

"By name."

Lance winced. That was a problem, to be sure, but not the type of thing that would get Roth driving across three states in the middle of the night. There was more coming. "Who sent it?" he said.

"That's what you're here for."

Lance nodded. He looked at the picture, it was of a man, and said, "Who's the stooge?"

"No one you recognize?"

"Should I?"

"His name is Daniil Grechko," Roth said. "He landed at JFK two days ago on a commercial flight from Moscow, ostensibly to work at the consulate as a translator."

"You think that's a cover?"

"Look at him."

It was true. The man didn't have the look of a

translator about him. He looked more like a nightclub bouncer.

"Kathleen's already confirmed he's GRU. Top floor."

"Reporting to?"

"We don't know yet, though she's working on it."

Lance looked closely at the photo, the man's face—sunglasses, dark stubble, the collar of a leather jacket. Someone had sent it, which meant they were trying to tell Roth something. But what? "Why don't you just jump straight to the punchline?" he said. "What's got you so spooked?"

"I'm not spooked," Roth said indignantly.

"Your face is pale as a sheet," Lance said. "You look like you just ate a can of bad clams."

Roth sighed, then turned over the photo to show the back.

Four words.

Mustang
Rebel
Camaro
Hornet

6

Clarice sat on the bed, fidgeting. She'd had a bad nail-biting habit when she was younger—bad enough to be prescribed Zoloft and Lexapro—and when she realized she was doing it, she stopped immediately.

Her phone vibrated, and she jumped. She was antsy. She told herself to calm down.

She looked at Grechko's message, the same one she'd already ignored.

Who is Mustang's target?

"Uh-uh," she muttered. That wasn't how it worked. She'd already given him something. *Quid pro quo.* It was his turn.

Is my extraction ready?

She picked at a fingernail until his reply.

Almost.

Almost. Almost wasn't good enough. He was toying with her now, stringing her along, doing exactly what he'd promised not to. She'd done everything they'd asked. She'd delivered the goods. Her mission was complete. That was why she'd orchestrated this jaunt to the city in the first place. It wasn't a romantic getaway. She wasn't a dolt. Grechko had told her to come so he could get her out.

She'd have preferred DC—this had the feel of another stalling tactic—but it had always been New York with Grechko. It was where he'd recruited her. Where they'd met, the two times it happened. It made sense he'd arrange the extraction there. "The GRU hates operating inside the Beltway," he'd once said. "DC is too small. Too closely monitored. It's easier to slip under the radar in New York." Which was true, and the reason she'd agreed to come. But he was still dicking with her. She sent another message.

I'm alone. Lance is en route to Teterboro. Timing is perfect.

Again, silence. "Come on, Daniil," she muttered. "Come on and answer, you piece of shit." She threw the phone down and got up from the bed. She went to the window, then to the coffeemaker, and made herself another capsule of coffee. She didn't like this feeling. She had no leverage. And the worst part was she'd seen it coming. She'd known he'd try this shit. That was why she'd planned for it.

"We both know how dice work," she'd said at that first meeting. "If you throw them long enough, you eventually roll snake eyes. It's a mathematical certainty."

"It won't come to that."

"It will, Daniil. Someone will get sloppy. Someone will shit the bed. Someone on your side. In Moscow."

"They won't."

"Roth's no fool," she said. "He knows what he's about."

"No one in the Aquarium would deny that."

"He's old school. If he finds out he's got a rat, even before he knows who it is, he'll clean house."

"There'll be time to get you out."

"He'll burn everything to the ground, Daniil. There'll be no time."

"He'll hesitate. He'll try to save the ship. That's when we'll get you out. Everyone's got a blind spot, Clarice. His is that he's sentimental."

"Is he?" she said skeptically.

"He cares about his people. It's a weakness."

Clarice chewed on that a moment.

Grechko said, "We'll get you out, Clarice. We look after our own. If nothing else, you can count on us for that. You have my word."

"Your *word*?"

"Yes," he said without any hint of irony, as if it was inconceivable he'd lie, inconceivable he'd hang her out to dry.

"Forgive me," she said, "but coming from the man who just said Roth's weakness was his sentimentalism—"

"What more can I give you?" Grechko said. "I'm telling you we'll do what we can when the time comes. If you don't trust me," he said, giving her a grand shrug, "I don't know, hold something back, why don't you?" She could still hear him say the words. "Keep something in reserve. A guarantee. Something you know we want."

She sighed now and looked at her phone. Still no reply. She wasn't the first woman to look back on a honeymoon with regret, she supposed. It was always the same with men. As soon as they got what they wanted, you lost all your power. It was her mother who'd taught her that lesson, not Grechko. "You have to know what they want," she'd said to Clarice, sipping her wine from a coffee mug at the breakfast table. "As long as you have what they want, you hold all the cards."

"How, though?" Clarice had said. She'd been too young for such talk, too young to know what she knew, but there it was.

"You're smart," her mother had said. "Some genies, once they're out of the bottle, are very hard to put back inside." She knew what she was about, too, Clarice's mother, and she was speaking from experience. "Dish it out little by little, girlie," she'd said. "Give it to them piecemeal. Hold back."

And that was the wisdom Clarice had sought to apply against Grechko. She'd tried to hold back, tried to keep a little something in reserve. She'd thought she was that something. Her body. She'd thought that was her ticket.

She looked at the phone again. Still nothing. Had she missed something? Had she misread Grechko? Had she already given him everything he wanted?

She cast her mind back to her second meeting with him. It had been just one night after the first, still in New York, at a college bar on Amsterdam Avenue not far from the Columbia campus. He'd been drinking. When she arrived, he was already half in the bag, tottering on his stool, obnoxiously waving a fifty-dollar bill at the bartender.

Clarice stood by the doorway a minute, watching him like a cat watching a mouse. At least, that was how she imagined herself. Why was he drunk, she thought? He knew she was afraid of a screw-up. Vodka had caused more KGB casualties than CIA vigilance ever could. Was he trying to scare her? Was that why he'd forced her to meet a second time? What was his angle? Was there an operational purpose for risking her life, or was it just about getting inside her pants? If this man was going to get her killed, she thought, she might as well find out sooner rather than later. It wasn't too late to do something about it.

She walked up to him, took the fifty from his hand, and stuffed it between her cleavage. Then she opened the top three buttons of her blouse and leaned over the bar, pushing her breasts up and together with her arms.

Instantly, the bartender was in front of her. She let him help himself to the fifty and said, "My friend's ready for another round."

The bartender grinned. "And what are you ready for?"

"If I see it," she said, "I'll let you know."

"She'll have what I'm having," Grechko said, trying feebly to stake some sort of claim on her.

The bartender disappeared, and Clarice sat down. Instantly, Grechko's hand was in her skirt. She pushed it away, then slapped him hard in the face. "I'm sorry," she said, "but what gave you the impression I'd let you anywhere near me without knowing what I'd get in return?"

He eyed her cleavage, and she wondered if he was really as drunk as he was letting on. It was an old trick, a great way of getting someone to let their guard down. She was pretty sure this display was genuine, though. "Why am I here, Daniil?"

"Clarice, relax. We're getting to know each other. That's all." He waved at the bartender and raised two fingers.

The bartender brought two vodkas, and Daniil told him to bring two more. It was after the second drink that Clarice said, "What is it they're going to make me do? What's my pound of flesh?"

Grechko smiled.

She looked back at him blankly, her gaze icy cold. This was it. Brass tacks. This was the cost of admission.

"Come on, Clarice," he said. "You know what they're going to ask of you. Same thing as always."

She gave no reaction, as if she had no idea what he meant, and said, "Why don't you spell it out for me?"

"Oh, it's nothing too difficult," he said. "All you have to do is lie there. I dare say you might enjoy it." He treated her to a toothy grin that revealed all the faults of the Soviet dentistry of his youth.

"If that's supposed to be a joke," she said, "you really shouldn't." "Watching you try to be funny is like watching a grown man putting on a tutu."

"Are you trying to hurt my feelings?"

"Are you trying to hurt mine?"

"Don't be like that," he said. "Of course they want a honeytrap. What else could it be?"

"I don't know," she said. "I thought maybe

something with a little more imagination. I'm handler to the most deadly asset in CIA history."

"This is really not that bad."

"Easy for you to say."

"You haven't even asked who the target is."

"I don't need to. It's Roth."

Grechko shook his head.

"Not Roth?" she said, surprised. She was almost disappointed. He was old, but then, so were her scars. It left only one candidate. "Oh no," she said, her heart thumping in her chest. One thing was certain—the very thought of it got her blood flowing. She felt her face flush.

Grechko nodded. "Don't play coy."

"I'm not playing anything. Lance is a trained killer. If he gets so much of an inkling—"

"Of what?"

"My true feelings, my emotions, he'll know something's off."

"Women are complicated creatures," Grechko said, as if he had any qualification on the matter. "He won't have the first clue as to your true emotions, your true feelings. He'll be as confused as a bull in a china shop. He won't know what he's thinking."

"He might."

"Love, sex, romance. It's the perfect smokescreen. Has any man *ever* known what the woman in his bed is thinking?"

"This is different."

"Is it? With your skill, Clarice, it will be a perfect storm."

"You're giving me a lot of credit."

"His head will be spinning. A hundred times a day, he'll go from thinking you're the best thing that ever happened to him to the worst. By the time he suspects what's really going on, you'll be a thousand miles away."

"I'll need to be a lot farther than that."

"This will be a brief seduction, Clarice. A quick in and out." He slid a finger in and out of his other hand.

"There you go again," she said.

"A hippopotamus learning ballet."

She nodded.

"Admit it, though," he said. "You want it. You want *him*."

She said nothing.

"Oh," he said, suddenly surprised. "You don't want *him*. You want to *fuck* him. And not in the good way."

"You don't know what I want."

"You dislike this man. You wish him ill."

"I hope the GRU isn't paying you for your psychic abilities."

"I don't think they're paying me very much for any of my abilities, to be honest."

He ordered two more drinks, and she was quiet while they waited for them. Then, when they'd arrived, she said, "One question, though."

"Of course," he said, taking a sip.

"What's the point of targeting him?"

"You don't expect the GRU to share all its secrets with a lowly defector, do you?"

"But," she continued, "I mean, it will be completely useless as *Kompromat*. He wouldn't care who knew about a dalliance like this. He's not even married. If anything, he'd be embarrassed he hadn't bedded me sooner."

"This mission is not about *Kompromat*," Grechko said.

"Then what is it about? Spector isn't a decision-maker. He's an operator. He's a tool."

"You said yourself that he's the deadliest asset in CIA history."

"But he follows orders."

"Exactly."

She was about to say more but stopped. She took another breath. "You want to be the ones giving the orders."

Grechko raised an eyebrow, then nodded. He ordered more drinks. Clarice's head was already spinning, but when the next drink arrived, she downed it in a single go.

"Me thinks the lady doth protest too much," Grechko said. "If I didn't know better, I'd say you're getting quite wet at the thought—"

"Fuck off," she said. "If I'd wanted to bed Spector—"

"Oh, you're not just going to bed him, my dear. You're going to get pregnant."

7

Lance stared at the four words on the back of the photograph.

Roth nodded. "I thought that would get you."

Lance swallowed. "That was on there when you got it?"

Roth didn't bother answering, just gave him a look. Of course it was on there. That was the whole point.

Lance looked out the window—they were making a right onto Park Avenue. He looked back at the photo. The handwriting was crude, difficult to read. If he had to guess, he'd have said it bore the signs of someone used to scribbling in Cyrillic.

"It packs a punch, doesn't it?" Roth said.

Lance looked at him. "It's a shot across the bow, is what it is. Someone certainly wants your attention."

"And they have it," Roth said, taking the photo and putting it carefully back in the briefcase.

Lance looked at Roth long and hard, trying to imagine what he was thinking. According to the lore, the four words on the back of the photo had been assigned by Roth to the very first assets over thirty years ago. Supposedly, they were based on the four cars the handlers had been driving at the time. Four American cars. Four American assassins. Very cute. Lance didn't know if the story was true—Roth wasn't generally one for cuteness, though who knew what he'd been like three decades ago. What he did know was that the assets were such a closely guarded secret that even the CIA Director wasn't read in on them completely.

Only the president and Roth were authorized to really know what was happening on the sixth floor, and even then, Roth kept the president on a need-to-know basis. That was how he'd succeeded in keeping things under wraps while working with seven consecutive presidents from both parties during boom and bust, war and peace, election, scandal, impeachment, re-election, and everything in between. In the age of leaks, hacks, and FOIA requests, this was one secret the US government had actually succeeded in keeping.

Until now.

Now, someone was saying they knew about it. In fact, they weren't just saying it, they were screaming it from the rooftops. They were throwing it in Roth's face as if trying to goad him.

"Could it be some sort of trap?" Lance said. "A trick?"

"What trick?" Roth said. "If they know this much, we have a problem, period."

"But our response—"

"There's no telling what else they know," Roth said. "We can't sit on this."

Lance nodded. His was the first name on the list. Mustang.

He, and all of the assets, operated under the constant knowledge that if their real names ever got into the open, the list of people who would want them dead was as long as the phonebook of a small town.

Things weren't that bad, yet—the codenames were only half the puzzle—but it wasn't good. It wasn't good at all. Lance let out a long sigh. There were no two ways about it. This was a big, steaming turd in the middle of the dining table.

If it was a traitor, someone from within their own ranks, then, for Lance, it meant putting a bullet in the skull of someone he knew personally. Someone he'd trusted. Someone he'd broken bread with.

He didn't relish that thought. Kills like that stayed with you after the fact. They lingered. They came back, unbidden, late at night when you were lying in your bed. If a man did enough kills like that, sooner or later, they caught up to him. Lance had seen it too many times, to tougher sons of bitches than him, to believe otherwise.

"This is why you didn't come through Clarice," he said.

Roth turned to him, and for once, the old man looked very much his age. "In circumstances like this, it's best to...."

"Keep the circle small," Lance said.

Roth nodded, and Lance could see the difficulty with which he said the next words. "If we have a rat—"

"Could this have been some sort of hack?" Lance said, cutting him off.

Roth looked at him skeptically. Lance didn't think it likely either, but he continued anyway. "Some sort of intercept? Something electronic?"

"It could have been fairies dancing in the moonlight, for all we know," Roth said dryly.

"Except it wasn't," Lance said quietly.

Roth looked very old indeed when he said the next words. "I don't think it was."

The car took a right onto 55th Street, and Lance said, "A rat then. We do what we must."

"And what would you propose?"

There were methods for such things—ways of dividing up your own people, getting them to chase shadows, seeing what information got flushed out on the other end. There were methods for smoking out rats that Roth was more expert in than anyone. But they took time. And they came with a price. You had to be willing to make sacrifices. Information. People. You had to break a few eggs, as they said. It was a nasty game.

"There are fewer than forty people in the world who know what those four words signify," Roth said.

Lance nodded.

The car turned onto Madison, and Lance looked at the driver. He seemed relaxed, leaning forward on his steering wheel so he could see the street signs as they passed beneath them. Lance turned to Roth. "We're driving in circles."

Roth gave him a bemused look. "Calm down," he said. "This isn't the end of the road."

"Why don't you tell me where we're going, then?"

"As far as we know, Daniil Grechko is inside the Russian Consulate-General on 91st Street. It's a few blocks from here. He's our only lead. I'm going to drop you off when we're done talking, and you can see where he leads us."

"You sure you trust me to do it?" Lance said.

Roth smiled, but there was no mirth in it. "That depends," he said, his voice a dry rasp.

"On what?"

"Are you my rat?"

Lance looked him in the eye and let a few seconds pass without saying anything—the old man really did look tired—and said, "If you thought that, we wouldn't be having this conversation."

"No," Roth agreed. "I suppose we wouldn't."

"You'd have come for me like a thief in the night. No warning. No talking."

Roth said nothing, and Lance let out another long sigh before saying, “Have you considered the possibility that whoever sent you that photo is trying to set you after your own tail?”

Roth shrugged. “I’ve considered it. It’s an old trick.”

“That photo could have come straight from the Aquarium. We’ve done worse to them, more than once.”

“Either way,” Roth said, “they know more than they’re supposed to. We need to find out why. If someone’s helping them, we need to smoke them out. If that means the house catches fire....” Roth let the words trail off with a shrug.

Lance nodded and turned to the window. They were moving slowly, not far from the consulate, and he pushed the button that retracted the privacy screen. “All right, Harry,” he said. “Pull over. I’m getting out.”

8

Clarice was jerked from her thoughts by the unfamiliar clang of a landline telephone. She stared at it blankly, over on the desk next to a leather-bound room service menu and a port for connecting ethernet cables. Either it was her imagination, or the damn thing was inordinately loud. She got up and snatched it off the hook, noticing the little flashing light that indicated a room-to-room call.

What was this now? Some fresh stalling tactic?

A room-to-room call in a hotel was about as discreet as a horse's head in a bed. Completely traceable. For all she knew, it would show on the room bill. *Was Grechko purposely scaring her?*

"Hello?" she said, sounding less certain than she intended.

It was a Russian accent that answered, though not Grechko's. "Clarice Snow?"

"Who is this?"

"A friend."

"I don't have any friends."

"Grechko told me to call."

"What for?"

"He said to tell you the Aquarium wants a handoff."

"A handoff?"

"The ultrasound."

"No way," she said. "Out of the question."

"They want everything in hand before they put you on a plane. Site three. Handoff protocol two. One hour."

"One hour?" she said, glancing at her watch. "This is the most ridiculous request—"

"It's not a request. It's from the top. Don't argue with it."

"He's stalling, isn't he? Why?"

"He's not stalling. This isn't his decision."

"I don't care whose decision it is. You're all tentacles from the same squid, as far as I'm concerned."

The man was quiet for a moment. Clarice thought he was going to hang up, but then he said, "Grechko's in New York. He's not stalling. He's here to bring you in personally."

"He's in New York?

"Yes."

"Then let me speak to him."

"You can speak to him at the handoff."

"He'll be there?"

"Yes."

"Why wasn't I told?"

"You're being told now."

What was going on? Why did they want a handoff? It made no sense. "What room are you in?" she said suddenly.

"What?"

"This is a room-to-room call."

"You don't need to know—"

She could already see it on the display—3820.

"Clarice! Don't—"

She slammed down the phone and stormed across the room to the door. Directly across the corridor, not four feet from her face was the plaque bearing the number 3820. She raised her fist and was about to knock when the door swung open to reveal a large, muscular man with arms that must have been at least as thick as her thighs were. She looked at his face. Dark stubble. Acne scars. He wouldn't be winning any beauty pageants. He wore black combat pants and a thin, skintight t-shirt through which she could make out numerous badly executed tattoos. Russian prison tattoos, if she had to guess. "Who are you?" she gasped.

He leaned into the corridor and looked left and right before pulling her into the room and shutting the door.

"I want to know exactly what's going on?" she demanded.

"Calm down."

"Who else is here?"

"No one."

"Is Grechko here?"

"Of course not."

"Then why did he send you?"

"He didn't send me. Moscow did."

"For my extraction?"

"There's more in play than your extraction."

"Then why am I being dicked around? I've done everything I was told. I've got the proof they asked for."

"Just one more piece of housekeeping, Clarice, then you're home free."

"Easy for you to say."

"They just need to set eyes on the proof."

"Do you know how much danger that puts me in?"

"Look," he said. "I know you're jumpy. It's always like this before an extraction."

"*Jumpy*?"

"Nervous, then."

"I wouldn't have to be if the Aquarium would just do what they said they would."

"This needs to be by the book, Clarice. They need to know they're getting what they paid for."

"They haven't paid for anything yet."

"They have bosses too, Clarice. They need to cover their asses."

She gritted her teeth. This didn't make sense. Grechko didn't need to be in the city, not for an extraction. Neither did this guy, for that matter. And if they wanted proof that she was pregnant, why not put her on a plane and get their own doctor to examine her on the other side? "Why all this cloak-and-dagger?" she said. "Why now?"

The man sighed. He took a step back from her, giving her room to breathe, and said, "Trust me, don't fight them. They're a bureaucracy. Let them go through the motions. Let them check their boxes. It's not like they're asking for something you don't have."

"They're asking for something they'll be able to verify in person the moment I step off the plane in Moscow."

"Look at it from their perspective. What if you got to Moscow and they found out you weren't pregnant? They'd have burned their most valuable CIA defector in a generation. Would you like to be the one to explain that to the Kremlin?"

Clarice shook her head. "A handoff is dangerous."

"Listen," he said. "A few more hours so they can verify what you've told them, then you're home free."

Her heart was still pounding, but it seemed to be slowing. She was growing slightly calmer. Knowing this guy was nearby didn't hurt—it was never bad to have an extra set of hands around if things went south—but she could also see the logic of what he was saying. Daniil Grechko, and by extension Clarice herself, worked for the GRU, not the SVR or FSB. The GRU fell under the purview of the Russian military, the General Staff, an organization of such colossal scale that it had no direct analog in the United States. By some calculations, the Russian General Staff was the largest centralized bureaucratic system on the planet, with decisions flowing from the top along a single, bottlenecked chain of command that was so cumbersome the Kremlin sometimes bypassed it completely. If the SVR and FSB—the KGB's successor agencies—were precision tools in the hands of the president, the GRU was more akin to a slow-moving sledgehammer. Clarice took a deep breath. A delay like this was completely possible. Who knew how many sign-offs Grechko needed before getting her out of the country?

But that didn't mean she had to like it.

She craned her neck to see around the man, no easy task given that his dimensions roughly equaled those of the passageway, and he stepped aside to let her pass. She squeezed by him into the room proper. It was identical to her own, but in reverse, and she checked the bathroom, too, making sure it was empty.

The man traveled light. For luggage, he'd brought only some metal equipment cases. As for *equipment,* it was laid out neatly on the king-size bed like an outfit he was planning to wear later. Clarice looked it over.

First on the roster was a PP-19 *Vityaz*—a Russian-made 9x19mm Parabellum closed-bolt Kalashnikov variant, capable of firing eight hundred rounds per minute at a two-hundred-meter range. Next up was a Soviet-era KS-23 special carbine shotgun and a selection of ammunition—the Shrapnel-10 and Shrapnel-25 buckshot rounds, as well as the solid steel *Barrikada* round, which could supposedly destroy the engine block of a car at a hundred meters. Finishing the roster were some *Zvezda* flash-bang rounds and two 9mm pistols, a Glock 17 and Glock 19, both with the trigger modifications used by the New York City Police Department.

It was a straightforward arsenal—the tools of a veteran who cared only about getting the job done. Clearly, stealth wasn't a priority. Neither was the need to cover his tracks. If he ended up using any of it other than the Glocks, he'd be giving away that there was a Russian connection.

"You're ready for a fight," she said.

He made a gesture that she supposed was meant to be reassuring. "Purely precaution," he said.

"Precaution for what?"

"To keep you safe while Grechko does what he has to do."

She arched an eyebrow. If that was true, then the more firepower he had, the better. She wouldn't have minded seeing a bazooka on the bed. "If Grechko dispensed with this useless paperwork," she said, "there wouldn't be a need for any of this."

The man smiled. She hadn't thought it possible, but it actually made him uglier. "If we dispensed with useless paperwork," he said, "there would be a lot in Russia that would be different."

She sighed. There was no point arguing with that, she supposed. She looked around for whatever other clues the room had to offer. On the desk, next to the phone he'd just used to call her, was a brown paper bag from a fast food restaurant. It had been torn open to serve as a plate, and on it were used ketchup packets, a half-finished hamburger, and fries. "They have room service here," she said.

"I prefer the hamburger."

She looked him over again, head to toe, and said, "I'm sure you do." Mixed with the fast food aroma was the distinct smell of stale cigarette smoke. One of the white porcelain cups by the coffee maker had been used as an ashtray. Next to it was a laptop, shut but plugged in. "Have you bugged my room?" she said.

He said nothing.

"I hope you have because if anything goes wrong—"

"Nothing will go wrong. Your man, he's out of town, yes?"

"Who told you that?"

"That he's out of town?"

"That he's my man?"

He shrugged. "Grechko."

She said nothing.

"It's not true?" he said.

She didn't answer. Instead, she gave the room a final look over. It looked good, ready for business, as if the Aquarium was preparing for her extraction as promised. "I should leave," she said.

"You'll meet with Daniil, then?"

"Do I have a choice?"

He shrugged again, as if he were completely innocent in the whole thing, as if he was, above all else, on her side.

"Will you follow me to the handoff?" she said.

He shook his head. "Not unless my orders change."

"Then give me one of the Glocks."

He hesitated, then said, "You already have a gun."

"So my room *is* bugged," she said.

He looked at her, then away.

"Which means you saw that little performance last night."

"I didn't watch."

"Sure you didn't," she said. He didn't respond, and she added, "Come on, one of the Glocks. It's the least you can do."

"Why?"

"I'm about to be extracted for betraying my country. An extra gun won't hurt my survival chances, will it?"

He looked at her a second longer, then reluctantly went to the bed and came back with the more compact of the two Glock variants. He handed it to her.

"The small one," she said.

He made to speak, but words escaped him, it seemed.

"It's all right," she said, checking that it was

loaded. "It's not the size that matters." She held it up then and looked right at him, her jaw clenched like a vise, her expression as flat as a corpse's.

She watched the fear cross his face—it was a flash, a flicker, like a glitch in a hologram. Panic ran through him like a jolt of electricity. She enjoyed the moment, letting him feel the adrenaline of it, then smiled, sweet as sugar. She lowered the gun and said, "Had you there."

"Hah!" he said, relief flooding his voice.

"Just for a second," she said.

"Very funny," he said, eyeing her a deal more cautiously than he had before.

"I didn't want you to forget how it feels."

"How what feels?"

"Being the one with your neck on the line."

"Oh," he said, still watching the gun in her hand.

"By the way," she said, turning to leave, "what do I call you?"

He hesitated a second, then said, "You can call me Arsen."

She nodded and opened the door but turned again before leaving. "You know," she said, "they're going to fine you for smoking in here."

He shrugged. "I don't pay the bill."

"No, Arsen," she said, then stepped out and shut the door firmly behind her. "I suppose you don't."

9

Lance went to the trunk of the Escalade and rummaged through a black canvas equipment bag. In it were a false passport and driver's license bearing his picture, a wad of US hundred-dollar bills, and a Beretta pistol with threaded barrel. There was a suppressor to fit the pistol, and he picked up the gun and looked at it—light, aluminum, chambered in the .22 Long Rifle. He put it in his coat pocket with the money and IDs, then saw a steel thermos also in the bag. He unscrewed the lid and smelled the contents—coffee, still hot.

He went back to the side of the car and knocked on Roth's window. Roth took his time pushing the button. When it finally descended, Lance said, "What's this?"

"Oh," Roth said, surprised, "I thought I'd forgotten that."

"Clem make it?" Lance said, handing it to him.

"Wouldn't you like to know?"

"Maybe I already do."

"If you did, you wouldn't pry."

"Is that what I'm doing?"

"Yes, and you wouldn't because you'd know there was nothing to pry into."

The window began to rise, and Lance slapped the car twice on the roof, sending it on its way.

He was on Madison Avenue, scarcely two blocks from the Russian consulate, but he didn't want to get there on foot. There were places in the world where a man could loiter for a few hours without attracting attention, but East 91st Street between Madison and Fifth—one of the most expensive zip codes in the country—was not one of them. If he tried to hang around there, leaning on a lamppost and looking nonchalant, someone's private security would be on him in a matter of minutes.

Besides, it was cold.

He looked up and down the street—it was utterly deserted—and noticed the doorman of a building across the street looking his way. "Hey, mister," Lance said, crossing the street toward him, "do me a favor, would you?"

The doorman watched him approach with a doughy look on his face, though he perked up when Lance handed him a twenty-dollar bill. "What's this?"

"You got a cab guy you can call?"

The man nodded and retreated into the entry

hall of his building. Lance watched him through the open door, talking into a beige-colored landline telephone. He came back and gave Lance an officious nod. Two minutes later, a cab pulled up to the sidewalk right at the end of the entrance canopy.

The driver leaned out the window, and the doorman handed him some money. The driver slipped it deftly into the cuff of his shirtsleeve like he was performing a magic trick. "Thanks, Willy," he said as the doorman opened the door of the cab for Lance.

Lance got in and took a good look at the driver, gauging whether he was the right man for the job. He had on a Yankees ball cap, tilted at an angle, and a checked shirt. The heat was on full, and the radio was droning sports results. Tucked into the corner of the rearview mirror was a tattered photo of the Virgin Mary. A set of rosary beads hung below it. Lance took them as a good omen.

"All right," the driver said, "where we headed?" Lance said nothing, and the driver glanced up at him in his rearview. "Buddy, you got a speech impediment?"

"I was just wondering if this is a busy time for your guys," Lance said.

The driver eyed him carefully. "You kidding? It's the middle of the night."

"Right," Lance said.

"So you going to tell me where we're going, or you want me to guess?"

"Not far," Lance said. "Just 91st."

"All the same to me, pal," the driver said, checking his wing mirror as he pulled into the street. They turned onto Park, and he said, "Where on 91st?"

"Just left here," Lance said. They'd only driven a few hundred yards since he'd gotten in the car, and the consulate building was already in sight, just ahead on the right."Would you mind parking?"

"You want me to park?"

"There's a spot right there."

"What am I parking for?"

"I was hoping you wouldn't mind sitting and waiting for a while."

The driver looked at him again in the mirror, this time with more scrutiny. "I hope to God you're not one of those weirdos."

"I'm not," Lance said. "I just need you to sit here a while."

"A while?"

"Could be a few hours."

"I knew it. The moment you got into the car I knew you were going to be one of those—"

"I'll pay you," Lance said. "A hundred bucks an hour."

"To sit here?"

"Call it two hundred," Lance said, counting out two bills. "Two hundred an hour to sit."

"And where are you going?" the driver said.

"Nowhere. I'm going to sit here with you."

"Is this some sort of—"

"It's not anything. I just need to be here."

"You better not start jacking off or nothing."

Lance raised his hands for the man to see.

The driver shook his head, but he reached back and took the two bills. There was a clock on the dash and he pointed it at. "It's a quarter after. I'm giving you one hour. That's it."

"All right," Lance said, leaning back in the seat and settling in for a wait. He opened his window a crack, and the driver turned up the volume on the radio. The commentator was still rattling through a seemingly endless list of sports results. The driver kept the engine running. It would have been more discreet to shut it off, but Lance didn't say anything. It was more important he didn't annoy the driver, and, in any case, it was cold and they needed the heat.

The spot was less than a hundred yards from the consulate, across the street, giving a clear view of the entrance. To Lance, it looked more like the entrance to a boutique hotel than any government building, with pruned shrubs in pots by the steps and a red carpet that crossed the sidewalk. A security guard who did double duty as a doorman stood next to the door with a radio at his waist. Lance could tell from the lay of his coat that he was wearing a holster.

The building wasn't large, a five-story Renaissance-style townhouse that had originally been built as a residence. The only approach was at the front along 91st. It had no vehicle entry gate or private parking area. There was a smaller door farther up the street, a service entry for staff and cleaners and the like, but Lance couldn't see a guy like Grechko using it. No, he would use the official entrance, as his station demanded. The only question was when.

The cab driver cleared his throat. "Hey, what are we waiting for anyway that's worth two hundred dollars?"

Lance had been hoping he wouldn't ask—the Russian government wasn't the type of thing people were willing to get themselves mixed up with for a few hundred bucks—and he said, "What's that?" as if he'd been dozing off.

"Who are we waiting for?" the driver said. "Better not be something illegal."

There were a number of other buildings between them and the consulate, and the driver seemed not to have noticed anything particularly interesting about the place. There was a Russian flag hanging from a pole on the second story, but a maple tree obscured the view. It was good he hadn't seen it.

"Nothing illegal," Lance said, with a yawn, trying to sound bored, lowering the stakes, downplaying any danger. "Just opposition research for a big divorce case."

"I knew it," the cab driver said. "Someone's getting his dick wet, isn't he?"

"You guessed it," Lance said.

"Who?"

Lance smiled. "Can't say."

"Anyone famous?"

"Afraid not."

"Not the mayor, is it?"

Lance laughed. "Some Wall Street guy," he said. "No one you've heard of. Believe me."

"Some guys," the driver said, shaking his head. "They just can't keep it in their pants, can they?"

Lance nodded. "And you should see his wife. She's an absolute knockout."

The driver nodded. He checked the time on the clock, then stretched extravagantly and hit the scan button on the radio. It settled on a talk show—a woman and man debating the etiquette of bringing dogs inside shopping malls. He scanned again and got traffic updates, then classical music. He pushed his preset button, and it jumped back to his sports results. About half an hour passed then without either of them saying much, until a sleek Mercedes town car cruised by. It pulled to a stop right in front of the consulate.

"Is this your guy?" the cab driver said.

"Could be," Lance said, sitting up to get a better view. "I won't know until he comes out."

The town car's hazards came on, and a tall man in a chauffeur's uniform stepped out. He walked up to the doorman of the consulate, and the two spoke.

"Sure has money, your guy," the cab driver said.

"If he didn't," Lance said, "no one would pay the likes of me to sit here watching."

"I guess not."

"Perk of being a regular joe," Lance said.

The cab driver laughed. "No one but our wives gives a shit who we fuck."

Lance leaned back in his seat and watched the driver of the Mercedes. He lit a cigarette and stood next to the car, smoking it. He was definitely waiting to pick up a passenger. "If my guy comes out," Lance said, "will you follow him?"

The cab driver breathed out through his teeth, as if he would have loved to oblige but wasn't in a position to do so. "Look, buddy—"

"It won't be far."

"It's not that, it's just, we talked about waiting. Waiting's one thing, you know?"

"I gave you two bills for waiting."

"Right," the driver said. "Two bills. It's... you know...."

They were both quiet then. Lance didn't care in the least about paying more money, but he needed to appear like he did, or the driver would get suspicious. "I really need to see where this guy goes next," he said.

"We're waiting," the driver said, "but following's a whole different ball game. People get awful angry if they think they're being followed."

"You'll keep your distance so they don't notice."

He breathed through his teeth. "Whole different ball game," he said again.

"How different?" Lance said.

The driver's brow furrowed as if he was doing some complicated mental arithmetic. He glanced back at Lance, trying to gauge what he'd agree to, then picked his number out of thin air. "Three?"

"Three?" Lance said.

"Yeah, you know. Following's—"

"A different ball game," Lance said.

"Exactly."

Lance said nothing for a minute. The chauffeur outside flicked away his cigarette butt and got back into his car. "Do it for another two," he said.

The driver knew he could get more than two. He'd gotten two just to sit there. Lance knew it, too, but the haggling was important. It would get him invested. "If this guy's important enough to have us out here in the middle of the night watching him," the driver said, "then he's important enough to pay three more to follow him."

"I don't know how much money you think I've got," Lance started.

"For all I know, this guy you're following is a serial killer," the driver said.

"You think I'd follow a serial killer in a cab?"

"I don't know who you'd follow."

"He's a stock broker."

"Says you."

Lance shrugged, playing it cool, trying to look like he was paying out-of-pocket. Someone appeared in the consulate doorway, but it wasn't Grechko. He came out onto the steps and looked up and down the street, then talked to the doorman.

"Who's that?" the driver said.

Lance shrugged, but he needed to seal the deal

before Grechko came out. "Listen," he said, "I'll give you three hundred to follow that Mercedes, but only if you don't lose it and only if you don't get spotted."

The driver wasn't convinced. "Where's he going to take us?"

"Who cares? There's no way you're making three hundred on fares at this time of night."

"If he leaves the island—"

"If he leaves the island, I'll give you an extra hundred."

The voice on the radio was running through hockey scores, and Lance said, "I'll tell you what. If Detroit beat the Rangers last night—"

"No way Detroit beat the Rangers."

"Did you watch the game?"

"No."

"Neither did I," Lance said, "so let's make a bet. If I win, you follow that Mercedes for three hundred bucks."

"And if you lose?"

"I won't lose," Lance said.

10

Jacob Kirov was a man who enjoyed his luxuries. His possessions, his only true love, included a 1954 Ferrari 375 America Vignale Cabriolet, even though he'd never learned to drive and hadn't the slightest intention of doing so. He also owned a twelve-by-eight-foot *untitled* Mark Rothko, which he kept in a pitch-black, climate-controlled storage locker at the Westchester County Airport. Or there was the seventeen-karat Tiffany & Co. sapphire fleur-de-lis pendant that had supposedly been gifted by Henry Ford to Marshal Philippe Pétain. He'd purchased it from a Buenos Aires art dealer specialized in Nazi treasure, and, big surprise, the Tiffany flagship on Fifth Avenue had declined his numerous requests to have it authenticated. No matter. Their refusal, which he had in writing, was all the proof he'd ever need as to its provenance.

His cellar received wine and cognac by the

vanload, smuggled through the Port Newark Container Terminal by an Albanian gangster named *Biçakçiu the Collaborator*. What he'd collaborated in, Kirov never asked. He didn't care. In one corner of the cellar was a three-hundred-square-foot walk-in humidor filled with embargoed Cuban tobacco. An eighty-year-old farmer from the Vuelta Abajo came by once a month to inspect the leaves and hand-roll panatelas and gran coronas.

To Kirov's mind, after the childhood he'd *enjoyed* in postwar Saint Petersburg—a time he recalled as an unending gray malaise of damp tenement buildings, watery soup, and brutal corporal abuse—whatever extras he indulged in now were the very least he deserved. The red satin slippers with gold tassels on his feet, the matching dressing gown emblazoned in gold thread with the two-headed eagle of the Russian Federation, the diamond-encrusted Piaget chronograph on his wrist—all were owed to him, were repayment of a debt.

His philosophy was that of a lotus eater. Every whim, every carnal desire, every bodily need had to be satisfied—indeed, *over*-satisfied to the point of nauseousness—before the opportunity was snatched away and forever lost. When he ate, he gorged. Greed was good, life was short, and fate was cruel, so get while the getting was good. That was how he lived.

And if any of his tastes made him appear ostentatious, too lustful of the things life offered, perhaps even a little more *flamboyant* than the strictly orthodox hardliners of the Kremlin would have preferred, then so be it. He was an old man. He'd put in his time. His *peccadillos*—as he liked to think of the unending stream of scandalously young escorts that came and went from his bedchamber—were a foible he'd earned.

God knew he'd paid for them and in more ways than one.

They said you couldn't put a price on a man's soul. Jacob Kirov knew different. And New York knew different, too, which was why the place suited him so very well. As Russia's Consul-General in the city, who better to enjoy what lay beneath its paper-thin veneer of Protestant, Anglo-Saxon morality? In New York, perhaps more than anyplace else on earth, he'd found that every vice, every depravity, every corruption of the soul, could be catered to. There was no itch they wouldn't scratch. The hotels had secret entrances. The restaurants had hidden doors. The back alleys had disguised delivery bays leading to illegal gambling rooms and opium dens. The underground sex clubs catered to the very rarest of rare tastes—*rare* being a euphemism for things that frequently crossed the line into the illegal.

Of all the city's gifts, the one he took the most pleasure in, the delicacy he found most delectable, as it were, was the whoring. In that regard, he was a glutton who knew no limit. He'd heard that New York had more Russian-born whores than Moscow did—male, female, and everything in between. One could be forgiven for thinking he'd made it his personal goal to know each and every one of them. In fact, in his bed at that very moment, he had not one, but two. He'd been told they were brother and sister, though he couldn't be sure it was true. They were young, though, and they certainly looked the part. He thought about them now, what he'd been making them do to each other, and cursed again the fact that he'd been called away.

How dare they, he thought, playing idly with the belt of his robe. Those whores weren't cheap, their owners charged by the hour, and the clock was ticking. If the blasted call didn't come through soon, they would be gone by the time he got back to them.

But that wasn't the only thing irking him. There was also a certain indignity to this task, a certain lack of respect for the position he'd earned. Being told to sit here by a phone at this ungodly hour was beneath him. *Something* important to *someone* was at stake, and Kirov did not enjoy being kept in the dark about it. If he had to guess, he'd have said it went to the top, the Dead Hand—no one else could have gotten him and Davidov to pussyfoot around like this—but he didn't know for sure.

He crossed and uncrossed his legs impatiently. He couldn't get comfortable. He was seated in an easy chair in his office, a tartan blanket folded on his lap, and he flung it to the floor. It made him feel like a cripple—like Hodgson Burnett's invalid in *The Secret Garden,* which was a book, incidentally, that he loved. He'd read it dozens of times, first in Russian translation, then in English. He didn't care that it was for children.

His office was on the consulate's fourth floor overlooking a quiet stretch of 91st Street near the park, and through the window, he could already see Daniil Grechko's car waiting. It was one of the consulate town cars, one of *Kirov's* cars, as he liked to think of them—a chauffeur-driven Mercedes S-Class with dark windows and diplomatic plates. Far too good for a common thug from the Aquarium, in Kirov's opinion. A ridiculous waste. What was Davidov thinking? The man probably drove a Lada back in Moscow.

But orders were orders, and Davidov was certainly entitled to the resources. Kirov looked at the roof of the car, the smoking driver, and chewed his lip. Something didn't smell right. From what he'd been told, the GRU was bringing in a defector. That should have been the simplest thing in the world for them. It wasn't like they had to kidnap her. Presumably, she wanted to be extracted. They could have sent her a cab.

But somehow, Moscow was managing to make the whole thing seem very complicated. It confirmed Kirov's belief that the Aquarium's new leadership was nothing more than a batch of half-wits. Worse, they were *parvenus,* upstarts—like Orwell's pigs. They had no idea of the sacrifices that had been made to put them in the plush offices they now occupied and no idea what to do with themselves now that they were there. They were a pack of grubby *Bolsheviks* trying to get their fingers on the Tsarina's pearls. Was this why so much pain had been endured? For men like these to wear Rolex watches and drink imported beer? It wouldn't end well for them, he thought, a brittle smile spreading across his face. It wouldn't end well for them at all.

He was snapped from this reverie by a sudden swing of the door. It was his housekeeper, a Belarusian grandmother named Aksana Itkina, who was shuffling into the room with a fully loaded coffee tray held precariously on one arm. She'd been making a fuss ever since the instruction from Davidov's office first came through—it was all *so very exciting* to be up and about at this hour—and she rattled over with her full china coffee service, the one reserved for special occasions, and a plate of fresh ponchiki. She put it all down on the table next to Kirov's chair.

"Watch it," he growled as some milk splashed from the little jug.

She mopped it up with a corner of her apron and said, "Are you sure I can't bring you anything else?" She spoke Russian with such an accent one would think she was purposely trying to butcher the language, and added, "I could light the fire."

Now, she was just getting carried away. "There's a cigar on the desk," he said.

She tutted disapprovingly but found the freshly

wrapped panatela and cut it for him using the silver guillotine the president had gifted him. She came over then, and Kirov leaned toward her as if for a kiss and let her put the cigar directly in his mouth. It was a little maneuver she seemed to enjoy; at least, she never balked when he offered it, and she followed it up by holding out the flame of a lighter while he sucked and puffed, trying to get the thing going.

"Are you sure they said four?" he said, taking the cigar from his mouth and checking that it was lit.

"They said eleven Moscow time," she said. "There was to be a meeting immediately prior."

"I see," Kirov said, glancing at his watch. "He's late, then, the bastard."

She nodded and hurried off, leaving him to pour his own coffee. He was just stirring in the milk when the phone began to ring, almost shaking his cup from its saucer with its clanging.

11

Clarice got back to the room and glanced around, half expecting to see Lance standing there with a gun pointed at her. Calm down, she told herself. *Focus.* Lance was halfway to Teterboro. What she needed now was to pack her things and get the hell out of there. She looked at her watch. If she didn't get moving, she'd be late.

She dressed hurriedly and checked herself in the mirror, wondering if Arsen was watching her as she put on her lipstick.

She grabbed her purse and searched the lining for a small rip. When she found it, she reached inside for the jeweler's screwdriver she'd hidden there. Then she went to the burnished mahogany cabinet in the corner of the room. It contained the minibar—the refrigerator had been built into it so that it all looked premium and made of wood—and she used the screwdriver to undo the four screws that held the paneling in place. This allowed her to pull the refrigerator out of the cabinet, its little bottles of booze rattling and toppling as it came loose. She reached behind it then and found the envelope she'd put there the day before.

She looked at it. Her name was printed on the front, as well as the obstetrician's name and the blue and yellow insignia of the Johns Hopkins Division of Maternal-Fetal Medicine. She was about to put it in her purse—the clock was ticking—but instead opened it and stole one last glance at the ultrasound it contained. Who knew when she'd have the chance to see it again? Not that it was much to look at, a fuzzy black-and-white image of a dark blob inside a lighter blob. She didn't have much of a maternal instinct—in fact, she still hoped the Kremlin would order her to abort the pregnancy entirely—but looking at the blob now, she couldn't help but wonder what would become of it.

She told herself she didn't care. She was neutral. Impartial. The fetus was Grechko's property. Lord knew it had been his idea. He'd even given her hormone pills from a lab in the Sverdlovsk Military Compound to increase her fertility. She had to be realistic. Travel light, she told herself. Trust no one. Feel nothing. Lance wasn't ever going to show up in Moscow for a game of *Happy Families*. He wasn't ever going to love her. In fact, if she ever set eyes on him again, it would mean either he'd found her to kill her, or the GRU had successfully forced him to defect. Either way, he'd know what she'd done, how she'd betrayed him, and he'd hate her for it.

A sudden shiver ran down her spine, but there was no use second-guessing herself now. She'd made her bed. Now she had to sleep in it.

"I'm not giving birth to a baby just for you to kill it," she'd said to Grechko at the second meeting.

"We'd never kill it," he'd gasped, as if the very thought shocked him. "Heavens, Clarice. We're not monsters."

"I know what the Kremlin's capable of," she'd said, ashen-faced, deadly serious.

"There would be no angle," he said. "The baby gives us leverage. That means keeping it safe. Keeping *you* safe."

"I'm not sure how much you think you'll be able to push a man like Lance just because of a baby."

"We'll find out, won't we?" Grechko had said, and she'd thought about it then. They really didn't know. Who could predict such a thing?

"You're playing with fire," she'd said.

"I'm used to playing with fire."

"Are you used to being burned?"

That was the last thing she'd said to him. That was how they'd ended the meeting.

She put the picture back in the envelope and put the envelope in her purse, next to her agency-issued Beretta 9mm. She was going to slide Arsen's Glock into the waistband of her skirt, an uncomfortable spot—she'd definitely have to keep her coat on to conceal it—but at the last second, decided to put it back behind the minibar where the envelope had been. Who knew? Maybe she'd be back. Maybe she'd be glad of it.

She reattached the mahogany panels around the minibar, then threw the rest of her belongings into her suitcase—it was small, she'd packed only what would be expected of a weekend away—and snapped shut its latches. That was it, she thought, looking at it. That was all she'd bring from one life to the next. Not a single item in the case had been brought for its sentimental value. What few personal effects she still had from her childhood—her mother's engagement ring, the photo of the two of them at Coney Island when she was eight, a picture of a golden retriever named Lucy—were still right where they always were, in the locked drawer of a nightstand in her DC apartment. She would never set eyes on them again.

It was no big sacrifice, she told herself—she'd uprooted before, cut ties, this was nothing new—but there was a nagging part of her that said this time was different. This time, it was a one-way trip. Like an immigrant from long ago arriving by sea, she would never be returning to her homeland. The town of her birth, her mother's grave, even the background noise of American life—the faces on the coins, the blue of a mailbox, the shield on an interstate sign—were things she would never see again. From here on, she would be a fugitive, a foreigner, a traitor in hiding. And she would be in

Russia, where there was snow on the ground seven months out of twelve, and her grasp of the language was rudimentary at best. She needed to be ready for that—her new name, her new identity, for walking into the grocery store and recognizing none of the brands. Those might have seemed like small concerns, given the circumstances, but she suddenly felt them with an immediacy she hadn't before. This was it. She was crossing the Rubicon.

She looked at her watch again. She was going to be late. She was almost there. One more hurdle, and she was home free. Grechko would call for a car to take her to some out-of-the-way airfield surrounded by cornfields and a barbed wire fence. That was how she imagined it, at least. She'd walk up to a GRU plane on a small private runway, she'd climb the steps, enter the plane, and poof, she'd be gone. And Roth and Lance would be left scratching their heads, wondering where they'd gone wrong, how they'd missed the biggest betrayal of their lives. She pictured it, the look on their faces. Maybe one day in the distant future, when she was lying by the pool of a Black Sea resort, sipping champagne and eating blinis and beluga caviar, she'd send them a postcard.

It took a certain kind of person, she realized, to do a thing like this. Normal people didn't betray their country. They didn't put their lives on the block. They certainly didn't get pregnant on the say-so of a foreign government. How had Roth missed this? It wasn't like he hadn't done his homework. He'd left no stone unturned, no record unaccessed, no witness unexamined. He'd looked at her from every angle, through every prism. He'd had psychologists, psychiatrists, behavioral scientists, and God only knew what else looking at her through their microscopes.

And all of them had missed this.

But of course they had.

They were fools to put their faith in such procedures. The truth was, no amount of vetting, no amount of desk research, could ever tell them what mattered. It could never tell them what had happened between a man and a girl in the darkness of the Pennsylvania night nearly twenty years earlier.

Roth knew the name of the town she'd grown up in, the school she'd attended. He'd seen the streets, the addresses, the school transcripts, and medical records. He'd spoken to ex-friends, ex-lovers.

But what could they tell him? About her father's death? About her mother's struggles with money, and drink, and men? What about what happened late at night, after her mother passed out and her mother's *boyfriend* crept out of bed in search of something extra? What could desk work say about that?

In fact, it was probably Roth who'd planted the seed for all this in the first place, she thought. That was how he worked. It was how he recruited. He sought out people who were alone in the world, people without families, without connections—orphans and outcasts—people like him. He'd forgotten to ask why they were alone. That was missing from his list of vetting questions. That was his blind spot.

Clarice gave the room one final look-over, put on her coat, a luxurious Burberry camel hair, and left.

12

Kirov snatched the receiver and growled into it, "You're late, Davidov."

"Jacob Kirov," Davidov said, his voice wet-sounding, like he'd just put food in his mouth. "I didn't realize things were marching to your beat. I hope my operation hasn't pulled you from anything important."

For the briefest second, Kirov wondered if the prick knew what he'd been up to back in his bed. Not possible, he decided, banishing the thought. "Aksana just brought in my coffee," he said. That much was true.

"Has the man gone out yet?"

"The *man*?" Kirov said, knowing full well who he meant.

"Grechko. The handler. I believe you two spoke last night."

"Briefly," Kirov said, which was also true. Kirov had had little interest in the man then, him or his mission. Of course, that was before all this high-level attention began piling on. Now, his interest was more than piqued.

"Well?" Davidov said.

"I can see a car outside my window now," Kirov said. "The driver's still waiting. I presume they'll leave shortly." Davidov said nothing, so Kirov added, "The plane's fueled and ready to go, too."

"Plane? What plane?"

Now *that* was interesting. How could he not know about the plane? He was the one paying for it, after all. "Grechko requested the fastest we have," Kirov said. "The ambassador's Gulfstream 7000. We had to have it transferred from Dulles to Saint-Hubert in Quebec overnight. All very expensive, I might add."

"I see," Davidov said.

"He had a budget authorization from your department, so I assumed you knew."

"I'll have to look into it."

"He said he has a defector to bring in. You knew that much, I hope?"

"Of course I knew *that much*," Davidov said stiffly.

"Well," Kirov continued, "he said he planned to get her into Canada before taking the risk of putting her on a plane. I can't believe you weren't abreast of all this?"

"These details are below my pay grade," Davidov said.

"The jet transfer alone, though, Davidov. With

all due respect, even you and I don't spend like that when we travel."

"Look," Davidov said with more than a hint of defensiveness in his voice, "there's a lot going on that Grechko doesn't know about. I need him to believe certain things in order for other things to happen. So he can make all the plans he likes. He can move jets to his heart's content if it keeps him humming to plan."

"I *see*," Kirov said, his interest rising by the second. There was definitely more to this operation than simply bringing in a defector. There was treachery afoot, and Daniil Grechko was in for a nasty surprise by the looks of it. "So you're saying things aren't going to turn out the way Grechko thinks?"

Kirov could practically hear the sickly sweetness creeping into his voice. It always did that when he was trying to tease information from someone.

"I'm saying nothing at all," Davidov snapped, which, as a statement, said quite a lot indeed. "And, lest there be any doubt, let's get one thing very clear. This call never happened, either. Am I clear?"

"Crystal," Kirov said. "Never happened."

"As far as Grechko's concerned…."

"We never spoke," Kirov said. "Got it."

"Not that I imagine you'll be seeing him again."

A silence followed then, and Kirov let it grow. It was Davidov's turn to talk. The Prime Directorate had set up this call for a reason, there was something that needed to be said, and it was time to find out what it was.

"Forgive me," Davidov said after the pause grew uncomfortably long, "but how much exactly have you been told about this operation?"

Kirov smiled. As if he was going to make it that easy for them. Hold your cards close. Say little. That was how the game was played. "Quite a bit," he lied. "This fellow, Grechko, is chatty for a GRU man."

"You'll have to do better than that," Davidov said icily. "I give you the favor of a courtesy call, and you repay me with games."

"Courtesy call?" Kirov scoffed, unable to contain himself. *Courtesy* was a concept that didn't exist in the universe of Evgraf Davidov. "Please!"

"Yes, a courtesy call," Davidov insisted.

"You were *ordered* to make this call, Evgraf. You're up to something on my patch, and the top floor wants you to get my say-so."

It was Davidov's turn to scoff. "*Say-so*! Are you kidding me? You overestimate your importance, old man. You're being looped in to clean up the mess. That's it. You're the janitor." He almost spat the last word.

Kirov made to reply but held his tongue. He still didn't know how much leverage he had, which meant he didn't know how hard he could afford to push. He had to tread carefully. "The Prime Directorate can make all the mess it likes," he said, stalling for time, "so long as it doesn't get blood on my nice clean carpet."

His mind raced over what scraps of information he'd been able to prise from Grechko the night before. He could have gotten a lot more if he'd realized it was going to be important, but it was too late for that now. What he knew was that the Prime Directorate was bringing in a defector. A female. Grechko had let that much slip almost immediately. Given all the nonsense going on now, it was safe to assume she was high-value, someone important, or connected to someone important. SOG maybe. Levi Roth's group. Grechko hadn't said so, but it was a pretty safe bet when the Dead Hand was involved. As far as they were concerned, Levi Roth was public enemy number one.

And her being female pointed to *Kompromat*. Kirov knew the game well enough to guess that much, too. *Kompromat* was to spycraft what sarcasm was to humor—its lowest form. Consequently, it was also its most common. And the most common form of all, the one perennial that never changed, was men putting their dicks where they shouldn't. It had ever been thus.

All said, though, that wasn't a whole lot to go on. Meat and potatoes stuff. Certainly nothing that would explain why all this fuss was being made. Could it be, he wondered, if the top floor was really fool enough to get excited over some lewd photos? Levi Roth with a secretary on her back? A gag in his mouth? Maybe some panties on and a gag in his mouth? It was certainly the type of thing he could see Roth doing, though he hoped that wasn't what they had. Surely they weren't so stupid. Photos like that would never turn a man like Levi Roth. They had to know that. He wasn't even married, for God's sake.

"Always worried about your carpet," Davidov said, still hedging, giving away nothing. "Trust me, we wouldn't be making a mess if it wasn't important."

"As much as I would like to believe that..." Kirov said coyly, still biding his time, still waiting for Davidov to get to his point.

When Davidov sighed, he knew he was getting close. "Grechko's going to have an accident," Davidov said at last.

"I see."

"He might not be alive for very long after his meeting with the defector this morning."

"Okay," Kirov said. They were at least getting somewhere now, though he suspected this was still just the scraps, things he would know soon enough anyway, just by virtue of their happening in his city.

"In fact," Davidov continued, "you might want to consider getting out of town yourself."

"That sounds like an awful lot of mess," he said dryly.

"Just for a day or two," Davidov said. "You and that housekeeper of yours," he added. "I know how close you are."

That was a slight. An insult. Davidov could go

fuck himself, as far as it went. Kirov had slept with more women in the past week than Davidov could manage in an entire year, chained as he was to his desk in Moscow. He swallowed his anger, though, and continued playing the game. "I take it the killer isn't one of ours?"

"Probably not," Davidov said. "If things go as planned."

Probably not? What did that mean? A double cross, certainly. A handler getting killed. It was unusual but not objectionable, *per se.* If Davidov wanted to get his own people killed, that was his prerogative. All the more so if the Dead Hand was involved. The question was why, though. What was his angle? What did it add up to?

"An American killer, then?"

"Does it matter?"

"It does if I'm the cleaner."

"All right, yes, the killer will be American."

"CIA?"

Davidov said nothing for a moment, then reluctantly, "Yes."

"You won't be needing my help, then," Kirov said. "The Americans clean up their own mess."

"There's more," Davidov said, his voice sounding steadily less comfortable as he got nearer and nearer the crux of things.

"More?" Kirov said, practically salivating.

"You know there is."

"More mess?"

"Possibly."

"A mess of our making?"

"For now, all you need to know—"

"Davidov!" Kirov snapped, putting as much bite in his bark as he could muster. "Tell me you're not looking to activate a Russian asset in my city."

Another pause, then, "Maybe."

"Maybe? *Maybe*? Do I need to remind you of the political tightrope we're walking here? The president has given explicit orders that the Americans are not to be provoked. I'm the policeman of that order, in case you've forgotten."

"We're all aware of the President's standing order."

"This is New York, Davidov. Not some backwater. There's an election coming up. The Chinese are watching. The United Nations is in session, for God's sake."

"That's why I'm giving you this—"

"*Courtesy* call?"

"Yes."

"Then tell me what I need to know. If I get egg on my face, you do too. Then we're both fucked."

"All right. I have an asset in the city."

"Wonderful!" Kirov said, throwing his hands up. "Fucking wonderful."

"Relax, Kirov. He's a good man. One of Suvorov's."

"What's his name?"

"Abruzov."

"Never heard of him."

"Arsen Abruzov. He's competent. Best of the best."

"He better be."

"I assure you—"

"Who's he going to kill?"

"That's the thing. Maybe no one."

"There's that word again. *Maybe*."

"It's a complicated situation, Kirov. Sensitive."

"He'd better not be one of those guys who leaves a calling card."

"A calling card?"

"Novichok. Polonium-210. Molotov's little clues that the Kremlin's been playing naughty."

"He's not one of those guys. He's very discreet. Strictly a guns and bullets man."

Kirov sighed. "Sounds *very* discreet," he said.

"It's Dead Hand business," Davidov said. "You don't need to understand it. Just do what you're told when the time comes." The line went dead.

Kirov put the phone down slowly. He sucked on his cigar and exhaled. Whatever was going on, he hoped, for their own sakes, the boys on the top floor weren't getting too clever for their own good. It would be an awful shame if they were to embarrass themselves. He rose to his feet to get a better look out the window. The cigar was burning perfectly, and he blew smoke against the glass.

On the street below, Daniil Grechko had just come out the front door. Kirov recognized him from his balding crown. *Poor bastard*, he thought. *He has absolutely no idea what he's walking into.*

13

Clarice hurried out of the elevator, scanning the lobby for the concierge. He wasn't at the desk, but in his place was a snoring security guard who looked like he was about to topple out of his chair. He had his feet up and was tilted so far back as to be almost horizontal. She strode up to him purposefully and cleared her throat. He didn't respond, and she did it again, louder, then rang the little bell on the counter, bringing her hand down three times in rapid succession.

That did it. The man nearly leaped from his skin and had to grab the side of the desk to stop himself from falling. He knocked over some papers in the process and swore as he bent down to pick them up.

"Ma'am?" he said when he'd collected himself enough to see her standing there.

She gave him a moment to wipe the drool from his mouth, then said, "I need a cab, pronto."

"Of course," he said, then noticed her suitcase and added, "Checking out?"

"No," she said impatiently. She had no intention of coming back to the hotel, but Lance was the one who'd booked it, and the last thing she needed now was an email popping up on his phone thanking him for checking out.

"Do you want to leave that with me?" the guard said, nodding at the suitcase.

"No, I don't," she snapped. "Just the cab. I'm already late."

"Of course," he said again, pulling himself from his seat as if being hoisted by a crane. He began walking, painfully slowly, to the valet stand across the lobby, and Clarice followed, practically stepping on his heels.

The valet stand was also unmanned, which was why she hadn't gone to it in the first place, and the guard leaned over it and picked up the phone. He pushed a button and waited.

Clarice watched, shooting daggers from her eyes. When he looked at her, she hissed, "How long is this going to take?"

He looked away, raising a hand and continuing to listen to the dial tone as if it required a certain amount of concentration. She fumed silently. Ten seconds passed, then twenty. "Oh, just forget it," she snapped at last, turning and storming off toward the exit.

The guard immediately chased after her, following her out the front doors and down the steps to the sidewalk on 57th Street. When she tried to hail a cab, he got in her way, insisting on doing it for her, and she rounded on him angrily. "Would you back off?"

"I'm just trying to help."

"You had your chance."

"It's just, at this hour, it's really difficult to hail a cab like this."

"Then fuck off and call me one!"

He backed away, nodding meekly and retreating all the way up the steps and back into the hotel.

Clarice forced herself to take a breath. She was more worked up than she needed to be. She was late, sure, but that wasn't the end of the world. Grechko would wait. It wasn't a matter of life and death.

Looking up and down the street was not doing much to calm her, however. It was worse than deserted, traffic practically non-existent, and while she raised her hand at the few passing cars, none of them were cabs. She stood there for five minutes, waving at every car desperately until finally, she threw up her hands in frustration. She considered going back inside and apologizing to the guard, a truly galling prospect, when a man in a valet uniform came out of the hotel and approached her.

"Your cab's on its way, ma'am."

"Where were you five minutes ago?" she said. "I've been standing out here like a complete idiot."

"I know, ma'am. I'm sorry."

"Don't ma'am me."

"No, ma'am, sorry."

"And stop fucking saying you're sorry."

It was another ten minutes before the cab rolled up, and Clarice fired off yet another message to Grechko, telling him she'd be late. It was against protocol to do so, but she didn't care.

Grechko didn't respond—of course he didn't, *the prick*—and as soon as she was inside the cab, she told the driver to step on it.

The man seemed to have at least *some* sense of urgency, and the car lurched away from the sidewalk, doing a quick U-turn in the empty street before turning onto Fifth Avenue. Traffic was light. That was a good thing, she told herself, forcing herself to breathe deeply.

This was unlike her. She was usually very calm in the face of pressure. For some reason, this meet had her acting like a little girl on the first day of kindergarten. She took another deep breath and went over in her head what was going to happen next.

The meet was at an all-night diner called Tom's. She'd never been there. She doubted Grechko had either. The protocol dictated that they both sit at the counter, one seat apart, so that physical documents could be passed between them if necessary, and they could speak with their backs to the world. Given that it would be difficult to get three seats in a row like that at a busy counter during the day, the protocol recommended using the site only between the hours of midnight and six in the morning.

It was ridiculous.

She'd have liked to wring the neck of whatever half-wit at the Aquarium had dreamt it up—someone, no doubt, who'd never set foot on American soil and who'd heard the phrase 'City that never sleeps' and taken it literally. Someone too, no doubt, who would never be forced to risk their life to hand over an envelope.

She remembered saying as much when Grechko first gave her the protocol list. "Times Square?" she'd said flatly. "Are they insane?"

"It's the spy equivalent of hiding in plain sight."

"It's the spy equivalent of shooting yourself in the face. The CIA would never do it this way."

"Well, you no longer work for the CIA," he said, his voice taking on a hint of defensiveness.

Clarice told herself now that it didn't matter. Just a few more hours, Arsen had said. A few more hours and she'd be home free, whatever that meant to him.

Despite that, her heart was thumping as the cab approached the garish blue glow of Times Square. The truth was—and this was a statistic she knew better than anyone—this was the point at which a defection was most at risk of going awry. She'd been spying on the most secretive intelligence agency on the planet for months, but it was here now, right at the finish line, that the horse was most likely to break a leg.

And a spy was most likely to get a bullet to the base of the skull.

14

Lance got a good look at the man's face as he came out of the consulate.

"That your guy?" the driver said skeptically.

The man was dressed in a tough guy leather jacket that looked like it had seen better days and loose-legged jeans of dark denim. His hair was thinning, he had a bit of a paunch, and altogether cut a singularly unimpressive figure—more like a Soviet bureaucrat than a Wall Street stockbroker. "That's the prick," Lance said.

In one hand, Grechko carried a hardshell briefcase, and he put it on the ground while he accepted a light from the doorman.

Lance had lost the bet, the Rangers had indeed beaten Detroit, but he'd managed to convince the driver to accept five hundred to follow the Mercedes. They both watched now as Grechko climbed into its back seat, shut the door, then reopened it immediately to throw away his cigarette.

"Looks like his driver likes breaking balls, too," Lance said.

The driver laughed, but he sounded worried, like he already knew he was getting into something he'd regret. He put the car firmly into gear and waited.

The Mercedes moved first, making its way slowly down 91st Street in the direction of Fifth Avenue. At the corner, it signaled a left turn and waited.

"Not too close," Lance said as the cab driver pulled out of their parking spot in pursuit. Traffic was light enough that even a taxi might be noticed, especially if the driver of the Mercedes was on the lookout for it. "Give them lots of room."

"What am I doing?" the driver said, indicating the wide gap between the two cars.

"A little more," Lance said.

The driver looked back at him. "You want to do the driving?"

"All right," Lance said.

The driver laughed nervously again. "Just pipe down and let me do my job."

Lance sat back and held his tongue. The driver gave more room, though still not as much as Lance would have liked. The Mercedes got caught by a red light, and they caught up to it almost immediately. As they sat idling, waiting for the light, the driver leaned forward and said, "Hold on a minute. Is that a diplomatic plate?"

Lance said nothing. There was no use denying it. The word *Diplomat* was printed clearly across the top of the plate. There was a country code, too, YR for Russia, though Lance didn't think the driver would recognize it.

"Divorce lawyer, my ass," the driver said. "What the hell is this?"

Lance took the money from his jacket pocket and counted out twenty bills, a full two thousand dollars, and put them on the passenger seat next to the driver.

"You better be kidding me," the driver said.

"That's two grand," Lance said. "You can give me ten minutes."

"What happens in ten minutes?"

"If we're still driving, I'll give you another two thousand."

"What am I getting myself into?"

"Nothing," Lance said. "This will be over before you know it. Just keep calm and give them lots of space."

The driver looked back at him, then at the money, then at the Mercedes that was still idling in front of them, exhaust fume billowing from it in the cold air. "That was the Russian flag back there, wasn't it?"

Lance said nothing.

"I suppose you're going to tell me to think of my country."

"I'm not going to tell you anything," Lance said.

The driver nodded. He looked at the money again, then reached over and took it. "Two thousand?" he said, putting it in his shirt pocket without counting.

"For ten minutes," Lance said.

"And keep my distance."

Lance nodded. The light turned green, and the Mercedes rolled off. The cab stayed put, just long enough for Lance to wonder if the driver was getting cold feet, then he pushed the gas, and they moved on, keeping a better distance this time. A gap of about two blocks opened between them, and the Mercedes sailed along Fifth Avenue, past the Guggenheim and the Met, through green light after green light. The cab followed perfectly, but as they neared the end of the park, the driver began closing the gap again. Lance could see why—with so many intersections coming up, the driver was worried they'd get caught on the wrong side of a light. "Don't spook him," Lance said. "He's not going anywhere."

The driver nodded, keeping distance a few more blocks as far as Trump Tower, but as they neared the Plaza Hotel, he began closing again. "He's going to notice," Lance said. "You're getting too close."

Just then, the light ahead of the Mercedes turned amber. The Mercedes sped up to get across before it turned, and the cab driver did the same.

Lance winced. "Don't!" he cried.

The driver put his foot down, the cab lurched forward, and the light switched from amber to red. The cab continued to accelerate, and then, at the very last second, the driver jammed the brakes. They screeched to a halt so abruptly Lance had to hold onto his seat to stop from flying forward.

"Phew," the driver said when they'd safely come to a stop, as if he'd been a bystander in the whole thing.

"Smooth," Lance said.

Ahead of them, along the length of Fifth Avenue as far as the eye could see, the synchronized lights switched from green to red, one after the other. The Mercedes had to stop at the next set.

Lance looked at the driver. His hands were gripping the wheel so tightly that his knuckles were white. "Listen," he said, "don't take any more chances. You get to keep the money either way."

The driver nodded.

"Just follow as best you can. It looks like we're going downtown anyway. It won't be much longer until this is over."

"And what then?"

"Then you drop me off."

"And then?"

"Then finish your shift like normal."

"That's it?"

"And tell no one about any of this," Lance said. "Pocket the money, but keep quiet about all this. Take it to your grave."

The driver nodded.

"I mean it," Lance reiterated. The lights all along Fifth Avenue turned green, and Lance said, "Nice and easy, now. Either way, you keep the money."

They moved on, continuing south for a few more blocks, both cars in the center lane of three. When the Mercedes shifted one to the right, Lance said, "Don't follow him."

"He's going to turn," the driver said.

"It's okay," Lance said. "Give him more space. If he signals, don't do the same until after he's out of sight. Then we follow."

It was ten more blocks before the Mercedes began signaling its turn. The cab slowed and let it round the corner before following suit. "Looks like he's headed for Times Square," the cab driver said.

Lance nodded. They made the same turn, and the traffic grew heavier as they got closer and closer to the glaring blue glow of the electric billboards.

"He's coming to a stop," the driver said.

Lance counted out twenty more bills and handed them to the driver. He said, "Real natural, now. Pass by him and stop at those lights. I'll get out there."

As they passed the Mercedes, Lance turned to watch Grechko getting out. He crossed the street behind them, hurrying into an all-night diner that was wedged between a Red Lobster and a subway station entrance.

The cab came to a halt at the lights, and the driver said, "All right. We're done."

"One second," Lance said, waiting for the Mercedes to pull away. As soon as it did, he opened his door. "You did good," he said to the driver. "Now go on, and don't look back."

The cab drove off, and Lance stood on the sidewalk a minute, sizing up the diner before crossing the street. It was still before dawn, but through the window, he could see that it had a decent smattering of customers. That was why it had been chosen, he presumed—a place about as near as you could get to being busy day and night, three-hundred-sixty-five days a year. There'd been a time when GRU handlers had preferred train stations and airport terminals for their meetings. That was before cameras and facial recognition technology took over public spaces, particularly in major cities like New York. Now they went for places like this—bars and restaurants that were pre-vetted for privacy, sightlines, cameras, and the like. The busier the place, the better, but nothing public, nothing monitored by police or government cameras.

Inside, Grechko was taking a seat at the counter, his back to the window. He was alone but took off the jacket and put it on the stool next to him, probably to hold it for whoever he was there to meet. He tucked the briefcase securely between his feet and picked up a newspaper someone had left behind. Lance wondered if the newspaper was the handover—it would have been an extremely slipshod way of doing things if it was, but it was possible. Anything was possible.

Where Lance was standing was the only place that gave a clear view into the diner. He looked up at the buildings that towered above him. None had windows with lines of sight. That wasn't a coincidence.

He tried to look casual, glancing up and down the street in both directions as if waiting for someone. He checked his watch, exaggerating his gestures, raising his wrist and pulling back his sleeve as if in a pantomime. If the GRU was smart, they'd have had someone watching the sidewalk. The last thing he needed was to tip them off now.

Across the street, an elderly woman with a scarf pulled over her hair stopped outside the diner. She had with her one of those wheeled carts older women sometimes had, and on top of it was a tattered shopping bag from Bergdorf Goodman.

Lance took out a cigarette to buy himself some time. He cupped his hands around it, pretending to have a hard time getting it lit, and watched. The old woman entered the diner. Grechko turned to look at her, then immediately turned back at his newspaper. The woman spoke to a staff member and then came back out. She still had her cart, still had her Bergdorf Goodman bag. Grechko hadn't gone anywhere near her.

As she struggled with the door, a man on the street stopped and held it for her, then went inside himself. He was wearing a loose-fitting business suit and a shirt the color of French mustard. In one hand, he carried an umbrella, and in the other, what looked like an old doctor's case.

Was the umbrella a giveaway, Lance wondered. It was cold enough that it was more likely to snow than rain, but rain wasn't out of the question.

Again, Grechko looked up briefly from his paper, then back down when he saw who'd come in. The host brought the man with the umbrella to one of the booths in front of the window, and Lance watched him take his seat. He passed right by Grechko's stool at the counter, but the two made no visible sign of contact.

Lance knew he had to move. If he stayed on the sidewalk any longer, he'd be conspicuous. The GRU might already have been watching. There was a bus shelter thirty yards up the street. He could stand there and pretend to be waiting. The first buses would be running shortly, but it wouldn't give a very good view into the diner. The other option was to go inside—he could grab a table, order a coffee, keep his head down—but that would be extremely risky. What if Grechko knew what he looked like? That wasn't something he usually had to worry about, but with a rat in the house, anything was on the cards.

An icy gust blew down the street, and he was half-tempted to get inside just to escape the cold.

A cab rounded the corner and slowed down. He raised his hand to get its attention, but it stopped just by the bus stop. He moved toward it as the passenger got out—he wanted to catch it before someone else did—but before taking three steps in its direction he came to a dead halt. In a sudden motion, he turned away from it, as if his hat had just been blown from his head, and ducked into a doorway. Keeping a hand in front of his face, he peered out of the doorway back in the direction of the cab.

The passenger had just stepped out, a woman in a luxurious camel-hair coat that draped all the way to her ankles. He couldn't believe his eyes.

It was Clarice!

15

Grechko glanced at the diner's single-page menu and went straight to the pastries. It was too early for breakfast. He didn't know how the other patrons were packing away eggs and sausage at that hour.

He looked around the restaurant—at the diners, the servers—everything was as it should be. He counted twenty-six customers besides himself, mostly singles but a few pairs and threesomes. Some men with hard hats and work boots were talking animatedly in the booth nearest to him. In the next was a couple staring indolently into coffee mugs. The woman looked like she'd been crying.

Grechko was the only person at the counter, and sitting there put his back to the rest of the room. Only the waitress could look at him from the front. From outside, the only way to see him was by looking in directly through the window. Anyone doing so would see only his back and would also be clearly visible to him if he turned around. From the buildings across the street, there were no direct sightlines at all, and the bus stops meant it would be difficult for a vehicle to idle for long.

It was a good spot for a meet—inconspicuous, busy, difficult to watch. He looked over his shoulder, made note of what he saw out on the street—vehicles, pedestrians, a dump truck—and would check again in a few minutes.

On the counter, someone had left a copy of *The Post*, and he picked it up and flicked through it. He looked mostly at the ads—Cadillacs for zero down, cell phones free with a commitment, kitchen appliances with no payments for six months. America, he thought, the *Land of the Free*. The land of the *interest-free*, more like. The land of the no-credit-check, low-monthly-payment, never-say-never chaos. He disliked it intensely, disliked what it stood for, but not for any ideological reason. Rather, he disliked it out of jealousy. He resented it, resented that Russia didn't afford him the same luxuries. If the CIA ever came to him with a defection offer, he'd likely take it. It was a decision he fantasized about frequently.

He raised two fingers to get the waitress's attention and asked for coffee and a bear claw.

"A what now?" she said distractedly. She already didn't like him. He could tell.

"A bear claw," he said, enunciating in his bad English and glancing at the menu to double-check. He pointed at it.

"Oh, a *bear* claw?"

"And coffee."

"Anything in it?"

He returned to his newspaper without answering her, leaving the question hanging.

She stood there a second waiting, staring at him, then turned and left. He was sure she rolled her eyes, not that he cared one jot. He was used to that. Waitresses in Moscow were no fonder of him. He rubbed them the wrong way. And not just waitresses, everyone. Arrogant, they called him. Presumptuous. Even as a child, people were quick to dislike him—schoolteachers, other children, even his mother.

He continued flicking through the paper—microwaves for thirty-nine dollars, a refrigerator for ninety-nine. Deals like that were unheard of in Russia.

The door opened, and he turned to see who it was. Not Clarice. He looked at his watch. He'd received her message. She was running late. Arsen also had eyes on her from inside the hotel. He'd confirmed she was on her way and that she'd gotten into a taxi alone and unfollowed.

The waitress came over with a mug of coffee and his pastry.

"Cream," he said without looking up at her from the paper.

"Cream?"

"Yes."

She glared at him a second, then left and came

back with a little bowl of creamers. She stood there then, glaring at him, waiting for something. He tried to ignore her.

"You're welcome," she snapped at last, storming off.

He picked up the sugar pourer and held it over his cup for a full five seconds, then he stirred in four creamers, opening the little cups with his teeth and spitting out the plastic.

A gust of cold air blew in, and he looked toward the door to see Clarice, wrapped in an expensive coat, wearing expensive shoes, carrying an expensive purse and suitcase. He'd gotten the measure of her from the get-go, he thought. She was a greedy, gold-digging money-grubber. And she was angry. At whom, he didn't know, though he assumed her father. They couldn't be trusted, women like her. They had no anchor, no rudder.

She came over and sat on the stool next to the one he'd placed his jacket on, never once looking at him. She tucked the little suitcase under her seat, and Grechko glanced at it. All packed and ready to go, he thought. Such an eager beaver. She'd be disappointed when he sent her back to the hotel.

They sat like strangers for a minute, he flicking through his newspaper, she scrolling on her cell phone, neither looking at the other. Clarice waved at the waitress each time she came close but couldn't get her attention. "What does it take to get some service in this place?" she muttered.

Grechko made no sign of having heard her—he

didn't look at her, and brought his hand in front of his mouth so that no one would be able to read his lips before speaking. Then, under his breath, he said, "You're worked up."

"Worked up?" she spat. "What did you expect? You're doing the one thing you promised not to."

"*I'm* not doing anything."

She turned to look at him, a breach of protocol, and said, "You're stalling."

16

Lance stood there on the street like a deer in headlights. He didn't know where to go or which way to turn. He was so taken aback that it literally knocked the wind out of him. He had to force himself to take a breath and then another, all the while staring at the door Clarice had just disappeared into as if it was a portal to another dimension.

How had this happened? How was she the traitor? Not one hour earlier, he'd been asleep next to her in their bed, her elbow in his face and the blanket in knots from her tossing and turning during the night. He'd brushed his teeth with her toothbrush that morning. Before leaving the room, she'd helped him into the coat he was wearing.

This made no sense.

He'd been completely blindsided.

He had not seen it coming.

That wasn't to say he hadn't tried—it was his

job to think the worst of people, to mistrust and suspect them, and he'd always given Clarice more than her share of that suspicion. He'd imagined a thousand ways for her to let him down, to betray him, to stab him in the back and twist the knife. This just hadn't been one of the outcomes he'd foreseen. It simply wasn't a path he'd have ever put her on. It was too dangerous, too dirty, too *distasteful*. It was distasteful the way a slaughter-house was distasteful—industrial, effective, but stinking of blood and shit and death. She liked the finer things in life. He'd never pictured her as a butcher.

He had to hand it to her. She'd kept this secret perfectly. For all her flaws—her mood swings, her coldness, her patent willingness to use sex to get what she wanted—Lance had had no inkling whatsoever that this had been lurking beneath the surface. What she'd been selling—her heady mix of lust and emotional whiplash—he'd swallowed hook, line, and sinker. He'd bought the whole damn bag.

What was it Roth had once told him? Nothing was off the table. Betrayal could come from any quarter, at any moment, from any player. There was only one rule in this game—trust no one.

"Like *The X-Files*," Lance had teased, though the joke was lost on Roth.

"You're going to see the honest man lie, Lance. You're going to see the believer deny his God. That's how it goes."

"You're a poet," Lance had said.

Roth shook his head. "Not a poet, a realist. Mark my words."

And Lance thought he had marked them. He'd thought his guard was up so high that no one would ever get the better of him. So much for that. Clarice had gotten the better of him the instant he'd let her pull him into that janitor's closet. The memory of it flashed before his mind now, her frantic, animal energy. She'd yanked his hair so hard she'd jerked his head back. Her teeth in his neck, and her nails in his back, had drawn blood. She'd thrown herself on him like her life depended on it.

And now, he thought, perhaps it had.

There was a thought—that the woman he'd been sleeping with these past months had been doing so under duress. Under threat. Had the GRU held something over her and forced her to do it?

Or, alternately, had the whole thing been her idea from the outset? Had she gone to them with a proposal? Had he been her price of admission, her table stakes for getting in the game?

Instinctively, his hand moved to the pocket containing the Beretta. Someone needed to pay for this, and with blood. If not her, then whoever had been pulling her strings. The man she was with, most likely. Lance slipped out of the doorway and pulled up his collar. Taking a risk, he walked past the diner window and glanced inside. Clarice had taken a stool at the counter, one away from Grechko. The two were sitting there motionless, neither looking at the other, like strangers, like ships in the night.

Lance didn't stop—he wasn't ready to give the game away just yet—and when he saw another cab approaching, he raised his hand for it. It stopped a ways in front of him, out of view of the diner window, and he climbed in. He dug into his coat pocket for his cash and handed the driver a crisp hundred-dollar bill. "Stay right here," he said. "It will only take a minute."

"What will only take a minute?" the driver said, eyeing Lance cautiously in his rearview.

Lance shook his head. "I'm not sure."

"You're not sure?"

"A... thing."

"Buddy, you all right? You look like you just saw a ghost."

"Worse," Lance said. "I just saw my girlfriend go into that diner with a guy."

"Oh shit," the driver said.

"Just let me sit here a minute and get my head straight."

"You're not planning on causing trouble, are you?"

Lance didn't answer. He didn't know the answer. He was still wondering whether the Russians had approached Clarice first or whether she'd approached them. Who'd initiated the whole thing? He wanted to know how much of an idiot he'd been. Had she seduced him with this in mind?

Had she been playing him like a fiddle the whole time?

"Buddy," the driver said. "Buddy!"

"What?" Lance said, his mind jolting back to the present. He could see that the driver was hunched forward slightly, leaning toward where he no doubt hid a weapon of some kind. "Can't you let me sit here?"

"You better not be planning on doing something stupid."

"Honestly," Lance said, holding out another hundred-dollar bill, "I don't know what I'm planning, but whatever it is, it won't be any skin off your nose."

The driver wasn't fully satisfied, but he took the money eagerly enough, and he could also see that there was a whole lot more cash in Lance's hand. "It better not," he said. "The last thing I need is trouble."

Lance looked over his shoulder at the diner. Someone else was going inside. They sat in silence a minute, he and the driver, until the driver said, "Just so you know, I'm blocking a bus lane here."

"Pull up then," Lance said. "To that taxi stand."

The driver did so and said, "We can wait, but we ain't cruising around after your girl like Ted Bundy when she comes out of that place."

"I know," Lance said. "I won't ask you to. I just need a second." He adjusted himself so he could see the front of the diner in the driver's wing mirror and said, "Something like this ever happen to you?"

"You mean, did I ever catch someone red-handed, as it were?"

"Yeah," Lance said.

"I got cheated on once," the driver said, then added, "that I know of."

"Then you know what it feels like."

"Wasn't like this. She upped and left. Only told me on the way out that she had another man."

"Did you love her?"

The driver shrugged. "In my way, I suppose. I was younger then. Younger and stupider." Lance nodded, and the driver said, "You love this one?"

Lance sighed. "No," he said after a minute. "I wouldn't say that."

"Then why are you so cut up? You look like you're ready to climb up a clock tower."

"Maybe I am," Lance said.

The driver eyed him in the mirror. "That better be a joke."

Lance said nothing for another minute, then, "Listen, I need to make a quick call. If you wait, I'll give you another hundred when I get back, plus whatever's on the meter."

The driver took a packet of cigarettes from his shirt pocket and tapped it on the dash. "It's your money, pal. I'll wait all day if you keep paying like you've been doing."

"Good," Lance said, opening his door. As he stepped out, the driver called after him.

"Just don't do anything stupid."

17

Grechko glanced at Clarice. The waitress had just passed again without stopping, and she looked ready to throttle someone. "If it's any consolation," he said, "the coffee tastes like dog shit."

"Oh, thank you, Daniil," she muttered. "That *is* a consolation."

He took a sip of his own and smacked his lips. She shook her head. He shouldn't have been goading her, she was worked up enough as it was, but placating women had never been his strong suit. "I know you're upset," he hazarded.

"Upset?" she spat. "I had one condition when all this began. One."

"I'm going to get you out."

"When?"

"Just let the Aquarium dot their t's and cross their i's, as you say in English."

Through gritted teeth, she said, “Yes, we’re well known for our dotted t’s.”

“The delay’s not coming from me.”

“Don’t you dare pass the buck, Daniil.”

“It’s not even a top-floor decision, Clarice. It goes higher.”

“Forgive me,” she said, “but do I need to explain to you the meaning of the word *handler*?”

“The Aquarium is a complicated place. There are layers upon layers.”

“Layers upon layers?”

“Exactly.”

She rounded on him, turning fully in her seat. When she spoke, it was loud enough that some people looked her way. “Do you think I’m a child, Daniil? *The Aquarium is a complicated place*? Are we all imbeciles now?”

“Keep your voice down.”

“You said you’d get me out.”

“The plane is fueled. It’s ready to go. What else can I do?”

“You can put me on it!”

He sighed, gave her a moment to calm down, then began, “I can’t do anything without clearance—”

She slapped her hand on the counter. This time, half the people in the place looked at her, including the waitress, who thought the gesture was for her. She came running over. “Listen, I’ve got two sections this morning. I’m run off my feet.”

“Sorry,” Clarice said. “That wasn’t for you.”

The waitress looked at Grechko then and nodded knowingly, like she'd be just as angry if it was her talking to him.

"I'll take more coffee," Grechko said.

She acted like she hadn't heard him and said to Clarice, "Anything for you?"

"Coffee," Clarice said. "Black."

"And me," Grechko said again, though again it went unacknowledged.

The waitress left, and they were both quiet. A minute passed, and it was Clarice who spoke first. "So?"

"So?"

"What happens? What do I have to do?"

"Well, first off, I'll take the sonograph, if you don't mind."

She reached into her purse and pulled out an envelope, in clear view of everyone, as if her recklessness was going to teach him a lesson.

He quickly folded the newspaper he was holding and placed it on the counter between them. "Put it in that."

She continued holding it in her hand defiantly.

The waitress returned and put a cup of coffee in front of her. She topped up Grechko from the pot.

"Thank you," Clarice said, still holding the envelope for all the world to see.

"Something wrong with the pastry?" the waitress said to Grechko.

He looked at her distractedly. "No," he said, "nothing."

She looked at him skeptically, and just to get rid of her, he took his first bite. He nodded approvingly. "Good," he said, spilling crumbs. She left, and he pushed the newspaper further in Clarice's direction. Clarice continued to ignore it.

"What are you trying to prove?" he said. "This isn't a game."

"Then why are you playing me?"

"I'm not playing you."

"This meeting," she said, glancing around the diner, "it's unnecessary. The ultrasound is unnecessary. Someone's making me jump through hoops."

"The ultrasound is absolutely necessary," Grechko said.

"Really? What are they going to do with it?"

"I didn't ask."

"Do you even know what an ultrasound is? It's a picture. It proves nothing."

"My order is to take it to the consulate. Someone wants eyes on the hard copy."

"Who?"

"I can't say."

She shook her head. "They're stalling, Daniil. They're up to something. And if you truly don't know what it is, then you should be as worried as I am."

"You're letting your imagination get the better of you."

"Am I?"

He looked at her, the defiance in her eyes—she definitely seemed ready to do something stupid. Something impulsive. He needed to give her a reason to keep playing along. She was still holding the envelope, still waving it around as if she wanted everyone in the room to notice it. What he needed was to bring her back down to earth fast.

He reached into his jacket and pulled out a photograph, putting it on the newspaper in front of her. She took one look at it, made to respond, then stopped herself.

"What's the matter?" Grechko said. "Cat got your tongue?"

She continued staring at it—eyeing it like a turd that had suddenly appeared between them—and cleared her throat.

He smiled. They could both see what it was—a photo of her quietly letting herself out of a Foggy Bottom apartment building, dressed in a skimpy black dress and holding a pair of matching heels in one hand. The side of her face was visible, but also the backs of her legs, and a run in one of her tights stretched from her ankle to the hem of the dress. There was a time stamp in the corner of the picture, though they both knew exactly when and where it had been taken.

"What's that?" she said.

"How you call it in English?" he said, taking another bite from his pastry. "The walk of shame?"

"Fuck you," she said.

"You just couldn't keep your slut legs shut."

"Don't call me a slut."

"If it looks like a duck and quacks like a duck—"

"No one ever said Lance and I had to be exclusive."

"Forgive me for assuming one cock would be enough for you."

"This thing's been going on for months."

"Months! Imagine that! And your life at stake if you got caught. I hope the guy was worth it."

She made to speak again but, for once, was at a loss for words. Grechko relished the moment, rare as it was, by taking another big bite from his pastry.

"If there's doubt as to the paternity—" she began.

"*If* there's doubt!" he scoffed, spraying more crumbs. "Clarice, please. You're smarter than that."

"I was careful that night."

"That night, the next night, how many nights were there?"

"You know how many."

"Do I?"

"Just that one."

He'd just taken a sip of coffee and almost spit it out.

"Oh, come on," she said. "What does it matter? I didn't realize the GRU was so prudish."

"I get it," Grechko said. "Lance was away a lot."

"He was away almost always."

"And you needed *satisfaction*."

"I'm a human being."

"And a vibrator couldn't have done the job? A

dildo couldn't scratch that itch for you? Or some spit on a finger?"

She looked for a second like she was going to punch him in the face, then she took a deep breath and said, "Look, I was careful. Every time, I took multiple precautions. Lance is the father. There's zero chance he isn't."

It was Grechko's turn to be sarcastic. "*I have your word on that, do I*?"

"Well, an ultrasound isn't going to tell you much, that's for sure. Not when it comes to paternity."

"I'm not a doctor. Maybe it tells them something."

"It doesn't."

"In any case, you'll forgive the top floor for making a few final double-checks before they roll out the red carpet for you."

"How many double-checks?"

"I've been told it will only take a few hours."

"A *few* hours?"

"One or two, max."

"You *promised* this wouldn't happen."

"As you said yourself, this has been going on months. What's a few more hours? This is the easiest part of the whole operation, Clarice. All we have to do now is wait."

"Easy for you to say."

"Go back to the hotel," he said. "You know there's a man across the hall. He's there for your protection. Nothing can go wrong."

"You did *not* just say that out loud."

"You're not getting jinxed, Clarice. Lance is out of the picture. No one's looking for you. You really are home free. Now keep your cool, go back to your nice room in the hotel, and order some breakfast. By the time you're done, I'll be giving you a call that the plane's ready."

She was quiet for a moment, no doubt mulling over her options, playing out the scenarios in her head of what would happen if she obeyed or didn't obey him. He didn't mind waiting. There was nothing else for her to do, nowhere else she could turn. He had her in the palm of his hands, so to speak. Right where he'd always wanted her.

At last, she picked up the newspaper, looked at it as if a headline had just caught her eye, and slipped the envelope deftly into the centerfold.

"Good girl," he said, unclasping his briefcase, scooping the newspaper into it, and shutting it back up carefully, with satisfaction, a job done. "I knew you'd see sense in the end."

18

Lance kept an eye on the cab as he dialed Roth's number. The cab driver indicated he wasn't going to leave, and Lance turned toward the diner. Impulsively, he walked by the window a second time, glancing again at Clarice and Grechko, who were still at the counter. Clarice seemed to have produced something from her purse, an envelope by the look of it, no doubt to be handed to Grechko.

He'd reached the doorway he'd sheltered in previously when Roth picked up. "Well?" Roth said, "Did you find him?"

"I found him," Lance said, looking up and down the street. "He was in the consulate like you said."

"And?"

"I followed him."

"Where to?"

"A place called Tom's Diner on Times Square. He's in there now."

"Who's he with, Lance? Tell me you've found the source of our infestation."

"I have," Lance said. "I've got your rat."

"And?" Roth gasped, exasperated. "Are you going to make me guess?"

Lance cleared his throat. It felt strange to have to say aloud what came next.

"Hello?" Roth said. "Are you there?"

"I'm here," Lance said. "It's Clarice."

"What?" Roth blurted.

"Clarice is the rat," Lance said. "She's sitting next to Grechko in the diner right this instant. Looks like she has an envelope to pass him, too."

"That's not possible."

"How is it not possible?"

"It doesn't add up."

"It adds up," Lance said flatly. "As much as it would for any of us."

Roth let out a long sigh, almost a wheeze, and Lance tried to picture his face—strained, tired, looking its age. He pictured him sitting in the back of the Escalade, briefcase open—ever at his post, ever ready for battle. He tried too to imagine what the old man was thinking. He would listen carefully now, to his voice, its tone, its tenor. The next few words would be crucial.

"I wouldn't have picked her for it," Roth said.

"Why not?" Lance said, probing, doing the one constant of their work—listening for lies.

"What do you mean, why not? I recruited her, for heaven's sake. I handpicked her."

Lance knew as little about Roth's recruitment choices as he did any other of his decisions. He certainly wouldn't have pretended to know his end game. He said, "So you're as surprised by this as I am?"

"Surprised? Are you crazy?"

"Maybe."

"You're suggesting I had a part in this?"

"We all have a part in it, Levi."

"This isn't one of my three-dimensional chess moves, Lance, if that's what you're insinuating. I had no clue this was coming."

"Okay," Lance said.

"I can see why you'd be feeling paranoid right now, but—"

"Paranoid? If I'm not misremembering, you were quite supportive of my getting involved with her."

"I wanted you to get your socks blown for once. Sue me."

"I seem to recall something about program design, too. About everyone being a bombshell."

"This has got nothing to do with that, Lance. Categorically, I did not get Clarice to spy on you. I sure as heck didn't tell her to defect."

"You're sure of that?"

"On my mother's grave."

"All right," Lance said, taking a breath. "No need to bring her into it. I believe you."

"You don't, but you will when you've had a chance to think it through."

"I hope so."

"I'm not saying I'm above it," Roth said, "but this one wasn't me, Lance. I don't have an angle in it. There's nothing to gain."

"All right," Lance said again, though he wasn't ready to put his suspicions to rest completely. They would just have to wait a little. His brain wasn't ready to do the mental gymnastics required to figure this through. "So here's where we are," he said. "Clarice and Grechko, sitting next to each other in this diner as if it's the most natural thing in the world. They're going to leave any minute, most likely separately, which means, at best, I can follow one of them. I've got a cab driver who already thinks I'm a weirdo, but I think I can get him to play ball."

"Let me guess which one you'd like to follow."

"Clarice!"

"No kidding, Clarice."

"Can you blame me? She's had me wrapped around her finger like a—"

"She had us all fooled, Lance."

"Forgive me for feeling a little singled out."

"I want you to follow Grechko," Roth said.

"She's got a suitcase with her," Lance said. "Looks to me like she's ready to jump ship."

"You know if that envelope slips through our fingers, we may never find out what this was all about."

"I already know what it was about. I know all too well."

"No, you don't, Lance."

"I slept next to this woman in bed last night. *That's* what it's about. "

"All the more reason not to follow her."

"Are you suggesting I can't be trusted?"

"You're *way* beyond compromised here, Lance. For all I know, you're in love with her."

"I'm not in love with her."

"You could do something stupid."

"Like what?"

"Like go on a shooting spree, for one thing."

"Don't tempt me."

"Or let her go," Roth said.

Lance laughed. "That's not going to happen," he said. He knew there was no use arguing the point, though, and not just because Roth was right. He was compromised. The truth was, the envelope was more important. Clarice—whatever else you said about her—had been neutralized as a real threat the moment she stepped out of that cab and got seen. From that point on, assuming she lived out the day, the only intel Roth would let her get within a million miles of would be chicken feed—that was to say, information Roth wanted the Russians to know, or think they knew. She looked like she was going to run, but if she stuck around, she was dead in the water. Her mission was over.

But the envelope was still in play. It had value, or the Aquarium wouldn't have risked a handover to get it. It was still an unknown. There were cases in espionage where knowing what the enemy *wanted*, what they were willing to take risks to *get*, was more important than knowing what they already had. This was one of those cases. If they wanted that envelope, Roth needed to know why.

"You've got to promise me something," Lance said.

"Do I, indeed?"

"If I follow that envelope, you've got to promise you don't let Clarice slip away."

"I've got an eye in the sky zeroing in on her location as we speak. She's not going anywhere."

"I need to talk to her."

"You'll get your closure, Lance."

"This has nothing to do with closure. Someone wanted me here, Levi. They wanted me to know she was the rat. This is personal."

"All the more reason," Roth said, "for you not to be the one following her."

"I'll get to her sooner or later."

"Lance," Roth said, his voice growing more serious.

"What?"

"You know this can only end one way, right?"

"This isn't my first rodeo, Levi."

Roth sighed, as if just coming to a very sad realization. "If it comes to it," he said, "if the next few hours circle you back into her orbit, and you have to make a choice..."

"I know what needs to be done," Lance said, feeling a sudden shiver run down his spine.

"She doesn't walk."

"I know the rules."

"You take her down, Lance. You take her down like the dog she is. You hear me?"

"Loud and clear."

19

"Anything else?" Clarice said testily, putting on her coat.

Grechko picked up the photo and gave it a final glance. "Who was he, anyway?"

"Who was who?"

"*Who*?" he scoffed, tapping the picture on the counter as if packing a cigarette.

"Oh," she said. "Him?"

"Yes, him."

"I don't know. A guy from a bar?"

"A guy from a bar?" he said, looking at the picture as if in great admiration.

"Yes," she said.

"A casual fling?"

"What's your problem, Daniil?"

"Oh, nothing," Grechko said. He could hear the peevishness in his voice as he added, "It's just, I would have thought, considering our *situation*...."

"Oh, no," she said, shaking her head vehemently, the contempt in her voice palpable. "Please tell me you weren't expecting to get an invitation to the party?"

"Of course not."

She gave him a long, withering look—a look he was all too acquainted with when it came to the opposite sex—and shook her head. "*That,* Daniil, was *never* going to happen."

He shrugged limply.

"And the guy from the bar," she continued, "if you must know, was nothing. A zero."

Grechko squinted at the picture. *Zero* was exactly right. A flash in the pan. Nobody. Grechko had looked into it in excruciating detail. He'd looked into all her little *liaisons* in more detail than the top floor would have required. The truth was, he'd been motivated as much by lurid curiosity as professional interest. He probably knew more about the flings than she did. "If it turns out," he said, "that one of these men is the father—"

"They're not the father," she hissed.

"I hope so, for your sake."

"I was *very* careful."

He shrugged. For what it was worth, he did, in fact, believe that. She was no idiot, certainly not suicidal, and the fact she was still willing to get on a plane to Moscow pointed strongly to her having held up her half of the bargain. "You're lucky the Kremlin isn't making you wait another month just to be certain."

She said nothing for a moment, then, "What

would be the point? They need me as much as I need them."

He smiled. She wasn't the first to make that mistake, he thought. He said, "You know, they can be very vindictive when they feel like someone's cuckolded them."

"No one's *cuckolded* anyone."

"I dare say that's not true."

"Lance is the father. They have the sample to prove it."

She was referring, of course, to the semen sample he'd ordered her to secure. She'd dropped it off at the Russian embassy in DC a few weeks earlier, and he smiled now at the thought of it. He hadn't meant to smile, but he had, and she saw.

"What's that?" she snapped.

"What's what?"

"Did I say something funny?"

"Of course not," he said, but the smile crossed his face a second time despite his efforts to suppress it.

"Oh, fuck you," she said.

He smiled again, chuckled, in fact, and had to cover his mouth to stifle it. "I'm sorry, Clarice."

"This is all just a big game, isn't it?"

"It's not," he said, struggling to compose himself.

She groaned dolefully, the same long, hollow sound she'd made when he first told her to secure the sample, and he thought back to it. They'd been on the phone—he'd been told, unusually, to make the call from one of the soundproofed quiet rooms in the Aquarium's cavernous underbelly. When he arrived at the quiet room, he found a team of technicians setting up in the observation room next door. This was before he'd fully realized how much priority was being put on the mission, and he remembered thinking that they were trainees on a learning exercise. He never imagined someone like Davidov was involved.

The phone receiver had been a heavy, old-style contraption connected directly to the technician's machines on the other side of the observation window by coils of copper wire. Through the glass, he could see them in their lab coats fidgeting with their controls, adjusting the settings to get everything just right. He said into the receiver, "I thought you'd be as eager as anyone to know Lance isn't firing blanks." Clarice had said something to the effect that that wasn't the point, and in a flash of theatricality that was wholly foreign to him, he added, "Unless, that is, you're enjoying the exercise." The comment got the desired result from the technicians, who he could see smirking, but it got the opposite from Clarice.

"I suppose that's your idea of being funny?" she said.

"Not at all," he said, "it's just, from the lack of results, one might be forgiven for thinking you were prolonging the process intentionally." She hadn't actually been trying to get pregnant that long—just a few weeks—but the top floor was already pressuring him for progress. "Our lab has confirmed you're fertile," he said. "Now they just need to do the same for Spector."

"Is it his fertility they're concerned about," she'd said, "or his paternity, once the time comes?"

"They need to know they're getting what they paid for, Clarice. No one's questioning your virtue. "

"It's not my virtue I'm worried about."

That was an understatement if ever he'd heard one. He'd recruited honeytraps all over the world—women who were willing to do virtually anything to get into the Kremlin's good graces—and even by those paltry standards, Clarice took the cake. She'd willingly given them the holy grail. She'd agreed to get pregnant. As Grechko and every other officer in the Aquarium well knew, in the thirty-eight years that the KGB kept records on such things, the pregnant honeytrap had been shown time and again to be the most effective form of coercive *Kompromat* possible against a male target. The only reason it wasn't used more frequently was the difficulty in obtaining it. Women, being what they were, had a natural aversion to the idea of using pregnancy as a weapon. Even those who'd demonstrated an almost wanton disregard to other societal norms proved reluctant to undertake it.

The relevant chapter of the GRU Training Bible, under the heading *Pregnant Honeytrap,* stated:

It is rare to find a man who will not bend in some manner to protect his own child from harm. This holds true whether the child is born or unborn, whether or not the man has met the child, and regardless of the circumstances of the pregnancy or the man's feelings toward the mother. Knowledge that the child was conceived purposefully as a means of gaining leverage against him does not negate the maneuver's effect.

The requirements to pull it off successfully are:

1. First and foremost, a woman willing to undertake it. This can be exceedingly difficult to secure by ordinary means, and threats are almost always counterproductive.

2. There must be no doubt in the man's mind that he is the father. If there is another potential father, the impact will be fatally undermined.

3. The man must know that his compliance with the coercive request will remove the threat to the child, but also that it is the only way the threat can be removed. No one else, especially the mother, can be seen as a source of protection for the child. This can be achieved by showing the mother's complicity in the maneuver, but if necessary, by threatening or killing her.

4. The threat to the child must be severe. In most cases, a threat of death will be sufficient. However, in those rare cases when it is not, then a threat of extreme and prolonged torture must be made and, if necessary, acted upon. All matters of scruple in this regard must be set aside.

5. The threat must be credible, meaning the GRU must be in complete control of the child. If the child has been born, having it institutionalized in a GRU facility is preferred. If the child is unborn, control must be exerted over the mother.

6. Finally, the ultimatum must be presented to the target in a situation of high stress, meaning there is intense time pressure, as well as knowledge that the decision will be final and irreversible.

If an ultimatum satisfying these requirements is presented, targets can be induced to betray their own side, even to the point of killing compatriots.

Grechko had memorized the section and appreciated that it would all have been impossible without Clarice's willingness to put herself in the necessary position of vulnerability. Ironically, the textbook also dictated that, as repayment for her trouble, she was to be treated worse, not better, than she would otherwise have been.

It stated:

The woman who enters into an arrangement of this nature thrives on abuse, mistreatment, and negative reinforcement. She is not in it for the financial reward, though such reward must be offered. Rather, she acts from an impulse to self-destruction, a nihilistic will to be recognized, even at the cost of her own destruction. It is a decision that will be made primarily to gain the attention of the men involved, be they handlers, the target, or whatever 'interested parties in Moscow' the handler can dream up for her.

Grechko had always known that Clarice was a rare breed, a one in a million, and that his primary role in the entire endeavor was to make her feel important.

"How do you propose I get this *sample*?" she'd said. "It's not like I can tell him to wear a condom, is it? Not after the fancy bit of footwork you did with my medical record." She was referring to a false diagnosis of polycystic ovary syndrome that Grechko had inserted into her medical record.

He'd also given her prescriptions for cyproterone acetate and an antiandrogenic progesterone, medicines she was to leave lying around where Lance was sure to see them. She'd left them in her bathroom medicine cabinet and also, when Grechko told her that wasn't enough, on the bedside table in Lance's Watergate apartment. The assumption was that Lance would read up on the prescriptions, find out Clarice couldn't get pregnant, and consequently agree to her suggestion they dispense with protection. All those assumptions had proven to be accurate.

"I hope you don't want me to jerk him off into a cup," Clarice had said.

"There are other ways to get a sample, Clarice."

"I'm all ears, *Daniil*."

"Ears, *Clarice*? Not *ears*, surely." He'd enjoyed the moment of her realization immensely. He even saw a few grins on the technicians' faces through the window. "That's right, darling. God gave you a mouth for a reason."

"How charming," she'd said. "So this is the Kremlin's official recommendation?"

"Yes, it is, signed and sealed in triplicate. Take him in your mouth, go to the bathroom, and spit it into something. I dare say you'll enjoy it. Just don't swallow in the excitement of the moment."

"And they say chivalry's dead."

"It's a little late to start playing coy now, my dear."

"What if I say no?"

"You won't. You're too eager. I can tell by the way you've been breathing into the phone."

She'd hung up on him then, but Grechko was so pleased with his performance that he'd gone so far as to give the technicians a little bow. They, in turn, gave him a quiet round of applause. The memory of it put a smile on his face as he finished his pastry and wiped his mouth.

20

As Levi peered out the window of the Escalade, the unnatural blue glow of the Times Square billboards reflected off the low cloud like an unearthly false dawn. A few flakes of snow had begun to fall, giving the strange scene an even stranger tinge. He glanced at his watch. They needed to hurry. They were on a dingy stretch of West 47th Street between the Barrymore and Samuel J Freeman theaters, and the buildings rose up on each side decrepit and dirty, laced in scaffolding and green safety netting that was coming loose and fluttering wildly when the wind gusted. Scarcely two blocks from Times Square, Roth thought, and the street wouldn't have looked out of place in a city under shellfire.

"That's the place," Harry said, turning into a multistory parking lot and stopping at the barrier to take a ticket.

"Let's be quick," Roth said, tapping his hand on his knee nervously. "Let's move."

Harry ascended the six levels of the parking lot about as fast as anyone would dare, accelerating along the narrow aisles, tires screeching as they took the concrete ramps from one level to the next. The lot was mostly empty, which helped, and they emerged onto a completely empty roof and came to a halt.

"Looks good," Harry said, yanking the handbrake and popping open the trunk.

Roth climbed out after him and helped haul out the black polypropylene drone cases. "Three birds," he said to Harry, "and three more on standby."

They had twelve drones in the car—low-cost, commercially available models from a Californian company called Skydio. The company worked heavily with the Department of Defense as well as fifteen hundred law enforcement agencies in forty-seven states. The drones were reliable little things, weighing five pounds and capable of deployment in under sixty seconds. Once airborne, they could maintain comms within a ten-mile radius of the Escalade or anywhere that had 5G cellular coverage, which was pretty much everywhere in New York. They had a forty-five minute flight time—which was why they were setting up backups, they could swap them out when the batteries got low—and a max flying speed of forty miles per hour. All in all, they were a good choice for car surveillance, and the only upgrades the CIA had made was for piloting to be routed back to Langley. Even the off-the-rack cameras, which included infrared sensors that allowed for autonomous follow, could read a license plate from eight hundred feet.

They set them up on the ground about ten feet from the car, switched them on, and then Roth pulled out his phone and dialed Clementine's desk. It took a moment for her to answer, and when she did, he could tell he'd woken her.

"Sorry, Clem."

"Quite all right, dear. That's why I'm here."

"The drones are ready."

He heard her rise to her feet, then she said, "The technicians are ready."

"Tell them I have three birds ready to go. Three more on standby. I want them on the front entrance of Tom's Diner on Times Square. It's two blocks from my current position."

"Aye, aye, captain," Clem said.

"Have them patch the feeds to my car—I'll lock targets manually—and have them arrange Keyhole coverage on the same location."

Keyhole, or Evolved Enhanced Keyhole, was the most advanced class of surveillance satellite the US Government, and therefore the CIA, had access to. The satellites were managed by the National Reconnaissance Office, which maintained round-the-clock operations out of Chantilly, Virginia. With a diffraction resolution of 0.05 arcsecs and an imaging resolution of 5-6 inches, they were just about capable of resolving a human face from their orbiting altitude of a hundred-fifty miles.

The height of New York's buildings created difficulties, but between the drones and the satellites, so long as the targets remained in vehicles and above ground, they would be trackable.

Roth and Harry got back into their car and waited for the first three drones to whir to life, which they did promptly, flying off in the direction of Times Square's blue glow. Roth still had Clem on the line, and as he opened a laptop and waited for the feeds to be patched through, she said, "I take it we've found our rat?"

Roth breathed in deeply before saying, "It looks like it."

"And? Anyone I know?"

Roth let out a quiet laugh. "You know it is."

"Are you going to tell me who?"

"You won't like it."

"It's Clarice, isn't it?"

"How did—"

"From what I can see, she's the only person on the team who could be at Times Square right now. She and Lance. And Lance is there at your bidding."

Roth sighed. "Would you have picked her for it?"

"I thought about it," Clem said. "I've spent the last few hours thinking about all of them."

"So have I," Roth said.

"Could have been anyone," Clem said. "Once

you know it's happened, you can see a reason why it could have been anyone at all."

"I suppose so," Roth said, "though I wouldn't have guessed this one. I wouldn't have pegged her for it."

"Not in her psyche profile?"

Roth didn't know if it was or wasn't. A person, a human being, was such a complicated machine that ultimately, they were unpredictable, despite what a psyche profile might say. Sure, in aggregates, human behavior could be predicted. How many people, for example, were going to die in New York City on a given day, or how many fender benders on the Cross Bronx Expressway, or how many iPhone sales daily across the five boroughs. You could predict things like that, and large sections of the CIA were predicated on such practices. What you couldn't predict, though, was what any individual person was going to do next, despite everything the shrinks claimed—and they claimed a lot. Every person, from the president on down to the lowliest pizza delivery driver, was ultimately unknowable. They could do anything.

"I don't know," he said. "Maybe I overlooked something I shouldn't have."

"You can't see a person's future, Levi. You can't know everything."

"Evidently not."

There was a pause for a moment, and then she said, "I take it you don't want all three drones for her, though."

"No," Roth said quietly. "Only one."

"And one for Grechko," Clem said.

"One for Grechko."

Clem said nothing then. They both knew who the third drone was for, though it might be unnecessary if he went with one of the other targets.

"He sounded surprised," Roth said, "for what that's worth."

"Never hurts to be safe."

"Right," Roth said, looking through the window at the ghostly blue glow of the mist. It truly did look like a false blue sun was rising over a false blue planet. "We'll see where this goes," he said. On his screen, the drone feeds were popping online.

Someone was coming out of the diner.

21

Clarice rose to her feet, ready to leave, and threw a five-dollar bill onto the counter for her coffee. "You don't mind that I leave first, do you?" she said.

The question was rhetorical. Protocol required that they leave five minutes apart, but Grechko knew she had no intention of being the second one to go. "Sure," he said. "Be my guest."

He gestured to the waitress for the bill, and she came right over. "For both of you?" she said.

"Oh," Grechko said, "no, we're not together."

She gave them both a look. "Sure you aren't."

She left, and Grechko turned to Clarice. "See what you've done?"

Clarice rolled her eyes. "And you put so much effort into your performance."

Grechko shook his head, took out his wallet, and rifled through it for some small bills. Clarice remained standing over him, and he looked up at her. "Well, what's keeping you?" It was the first time he'd let his gaze linger on her for more than a few seconds, the first time, in fact, he'd gotten a good look at her face since her initial recruitment, and he'd almost forgotten how young she was. And beautiful.

When she spoke, her tone had changed, suddenly earnest, like she was finally ready to drop the bravado. She said, "Daniil, why *really* are you in New York?"

It was a good question, one he didn't rightly know the answer to, and he said, "You know why. I'm your handler."

She waved a hand, as if to encompass the entire situation, and said, "You couldn't have handled all this from Moscow?"

"Some things require a personal touch," he said weakly. He knew it wouldn't satisfy her.

"And that's why your man Arsen is here too, is it?"

He wanted to say yes, but the truth was, Arsen wasn't his man. He was Davidov's. This was Davidov's mission. Everything that was happening was at Davidov's bidding. He felt a sudden shiver on his spine, as if someone had just walked on his grave, and said, "What are you trying to say, Clarice?"

She looked at him, long and silent and sad, and they both knew she didn't need to say anything. It was all there before them. All the evidence they would ever need.

Why had the top floor requested a physical

copy of the sonograph? It wasn't a paternity test. As far as Grechko was aware, there were two tests that could prove paternity—amniocentesis and chorionic villus sampling. Both required the mother to be nine weeks pregnant, which Clarice was not, and neither required possession of a sonograph.

The truth—and she'd been telling him this, one way or another, since the moment she'd walked through the door—was that something wasn't right, someone was up to something, and it wasn't just she who was in danger.

What she didn't know, and what he did, was who was behind it. He'd tried to ignore it, but he knew.

Why had he been ordered to get the sonograph in person? Why did they want it brought to the consulate? The consulate could protect it, certainly. Diplomatic custom meant it would be out of reach of any meddling American agency, but to what end? No American agency knew it existed. No one was looking for it. Even if it landed on their desk with a bow tied around it, they wouldn't have known what to do with it.

They had a saying in poker—if you don't know who the sucker is at the table, then stop playing and walk away. It's you.

Grechko was beginning to get the very uncomfortable feeling that he was the sucker. He was the patsy.

Clarice was looking at him, as if on the brink of

saying something more, then she looked away suddenly.

"What?" he said. "Say it if you're going to say it."

She thought for a second, then leaned down as if to give him a kiss on the cheek. She came in close enough for him to smell her perfume, smell the shampoo in her hair, and whispered, "I'm not the only one who's being dicked around here, Daniil."

And then, just like that, she was gone, leaving him staring at the door after her like a child who'd just been left alone in the dark. He continued to stare, lost in thought until he was brought back to the present by the waitress with his bill.

He sighed as he read it—a little printout, two bucks for the coffee, three for the pastry, plus tax. Had he just walked into the biggest trap of his career, he wondered. Had he just pulled down his pants and grabbed hold of his ankles?

He didn't know for certain, it could still go his way. All his fears could be nothing more than a chimera, an illusion conjured by the natural paranoia of a man in his position. It could all be nothing. But he certainly did have a feeling like he was standing on ice in the middle of a lake and had just heard a loud crack. He pulled out his phone and tapped a message to the driver.

Come get me.

Then he counted out three singles from his wallet and placed them on top of the five Clarice had left. He glanced at the waitress across the room and muttered, "*Fuck your tip.*"

22

Lance got back into the cab and sat down.

"Decided what you want to do?" the driver said.

"More or less," Lance said, though he still wasn't sure of the man's appetite for adventure. If he asked him to follow Grechko, would he do it? As a rule, if someone was going to refuse something, he preferred not to ask. This guy had been fairly amenable, the hundred dollar bills didn't hurt, but Lance wasn't even certain following was the right call.

The objective was the envelope, not Grechko himself, and that meant getting it before it disappeared into the consulate. Once in there, and then hidden away in some diplomatic pouch with a thousand other documents, it would be lost for good.

But the consulate was a very short drive away. An ambush *en route* might not be possible. And a diplomatic incident on the doorstep of the consulate wouldn't serve anyone's purpose, least of all Roth's.

That left an ambush here as the best option.

Lance was thinking through what that would look like when the driver adjusted his mirror and said, "Uh oh, looks like a lady coming out now."

Lance kept his head down as he looked out the rear windshield. There she was, the one and only, looking like the cat that got the cream.

"That your lady friend?"

"That's her," Lance said.

"She's looking for a cab," the driver said, adjusting his mirror again. Lance thought, if the man ever wanted a career change, Roth could use him for stakeouts. "She's looking at *this* cab," the driver added.

"Oh, no," Lance said. "Pull away. Go to the intersection." He could just picture the look on Clarice's face as she opened the door and found him sitting there.

The driver pulled ahead fifty yards or so, as far as the intersection, and Clarice shifted her attention in the other direction. It didn't take long for a cab to stop for her, and as she climbed in, Lance wondered briefly if he would ever set eyes on her again. It was possible he wouldn't, despite Roth's promise. If letting her go served the old man's purposes better than bringing her in—if she managed to slip away before the envelope was safely in hand, for instance—then that was what would happen.

"Now what?" the driver said. "This is a bus lane. We're going to get honked at when they come."

"Just another minute," Lance said. It wouldn't be long now until Grechko came out, too. One way or another, he needed to make a decision. "By the way," he said to the driver, "if I asked you to follow the guy—"

"The guy? I'd have thought the girl."

"I know where she's going," Lance said. "It's him I'd like to know more about."

"That sounds like a great idea," the driver said sarcastically. "I lead you to his house, and next thing I know, I've got two policemen at my front door asking what I know about some enraged husband who's gone on a killing spree."

"Come on, it's not like that."

"That's what you would say."

"And it's what I am saying," Lance said, reaching into his pocket for the wad of cash. He was about to hand over another hundred bucks when he saw the consulate's impeccable Mercedes Benz round the corner behind them. It came to a halt outside the diner, and Lance waited for Grechko to come out to it. Ten seconds passed. Thirty. A minute.

Lance was out of the cab before he fully knew what he was doing, hurriedly shoving two bills into the driver's hand on his way. Acting entirely on impulse, he strode purposefully toward the

Mercedes. He walked on the road, keeping to the driver's side of the vehicle, which meant he was out of sight from the diner, and rapped hard on the window when he reached it.

The driver of the Mercedes opened his window agitatedly. "What the fuck?" he grunted in a heavy Russian accent.

Lance had his hand in his jacket, and he took it out just enough to show the driver the handle of his gun.

"Oh, shit," the driver said.

"That's right," Lance said. "Now, we're going to do this real nice. No one's getting hurt. Unlock the back."

The doors clicked open, and Lance got into the backseat, directly behind the driver. "Give me your phone," he said.

The driver handed the phone back, and a minute later, Grechko appeared in the doorway of the diner, stuffing his wallet into his pocket.

"No heroics, now," Lance said. "No signals. Understood?"

"Understood."

"We're picking him up just like normal."

23

As night gave way to the first red streaks of dawn, a G-Class Mercedes wagon rolled up in front of the Midtown Four Seasons Hotel and came to an abrupt halt. It stood there for a minute idling as if making up its mind, then the engine cut out, and the front doors opened. Moving in unison, as if they'd practiced beforehand, two men in long black coats climbed out of the car and went to the trunk, where they hauled out two heavy-looking duffel bags and slung them over their shoulders. Without speaking, they proceeded up the steps of the hotel and into the lobby.

At first glance, there was little to differentiate the two of them, who cut nearly identical silhouettes in their coats, boots, and black leather gloves. In the light of the lobby, however, some differences began to become apparent. The driver, who was the taller of the two, though only by a fraction, wore a symmetrical pair of wire-rimmed glasses that gave him a vaguely intelligentsia look, like John Lennon in the seventies. As he passed the unmanned valet's post, he threw down the key for the Mercedes without stopping. The second man, struggling to keep up, was broader and heavier. He had thick, bushy eyebrows, like someone had gone at him with a black Sharpie as a prank, and dark stubble that extended from the top of his cheekbones all the way into the neckline of his shirt. It gave the impression of continuing unabated down into his chest and beyond.

They didn't seem in a particular hurry, though they crossed the lobby in long strides that ate up the distance too quickly for the bellhop to intercept them. "Help with your bags, gentlemen?" he called out.

"Get lost," the man in glasses said in a thick Slavic accent.

The bellhop cut a wordless retreat, backing away as if from a king and leaving the guard at the front desk to face them alone. The guard rose to his feet manfully, saying, "Welcome, gentlemen."

In barely comprehensible English, the man in glasses said, "We check in."

"Certainly," the guard said, glancing ruefully at the clock on his desk—fifteen minutes to shift change—then shaking the mouse to wake up the computer. "And do we have a reservation?"

The man in glasses continued doing the talking. "We have reservation."

"And the name?"

"Name is Neeson."

"Neeson?" the guard said dubiously.

"Liam Neeson," the man said, betraying not a hint of irony.

The guard nodded slowly, then hit a few keys on his keyboard and winced when he saw the results. "I'm sorry," he said, "but I don't seem to have a reservation under that name."

"No?" the man said, shifting the strap of his duffel bag on his shoulder and leaning over the desk so that he might get a look at the computer screen.

The guard instinctively turned it away from him and said, "Perhaps it was made under another name?"

The man turned to his companion, and the two spoke. The companion pulled out a cell phone and made a quick call. The conversation was in Russian, but the words "Liam Neeson" were definitely said. He hung up, and the two spoke again. Then, the man in glasses turned to the guard and said, "Check the name, Farrell."

The guard hit some more keys on the keyboard and, in a flood of relief, said, "Ah yes, here we go. Colin Farrell, two rooms, as requested. I'll need to see some ID and a credit card."

More words were exchanged, and it was the one with the eyebrows who produced two burgundy passports from a pocket in his coat and slapped them on the desk, along with a credit card.

The guard picked up the card first, a US dollar-denominated visa issued by Sberbank, the largest bank in Russia, and examined it, front and back.

"Card is good," the man in glasses said.

The guard nodded, then got up and brought it to the little office behind the desk. He returned a moment later with a printout and sat back down. Then he swiped the card through a terminal and said, "You want both rooms on this card?"

"Yes," the man in glasses said.

The guard looked at the passports next. "According to these, you're both Irish?"

"Yes, Irish," the man said.

The guard arched an eyebrow. "Both of you?"

"Both," the man said firmly.

The guard repeated the process of retreating to the office to make a copy, and when he returned, the two men were speaking again in Russian. The guard recognized a few words. "*Da, da, da,*" the man in glasses was saying. "*Irlandskiy, Irlandskiy.*" The man with the eyebrows was clearly agitated.

"Is everything all right?" the guard said.

The man in glasses turned to the guard and said, "He says you ask too many questions."

"Oh," the guard said, taken aback.

"You're not fucking police, he says."

The guard felt his face turn pale. He knew he should say something, but no words came from his mouth. Instead, he turned back to his computer, clacked on his keyboard, and finished the check-in process as quickly as he could. Taking two keycards from a drawer in the desk, he said, "Rooms 3817 and

3821, as requested." He put them in their little paper folders and wrote the room numbers on the inside flap.

"Good," the man in glasses said as he took them.

"They're not connecting," the guard said.

"What?"

"The rooms," the guard said, immediately regretting that he'd said anything. "It doesn't matter."

"What rooms?"

"We have rooms with connecting doors," the guard said. "That's usually what people want when they request two rooms by number."

"So what?"

"That's all I was saying," the guard said. "The rooms you requested are on the same floor, but they don't connect. There's a room between them."

"I see," the man in glasses said. The other spoke up again, and they had a little back and forth. The man in glasses said to the guard, "He wants to know if he look homosexual to you?"

"What?" the guard said.

"Does he look homosexual?" the man said again.

"No, of course not," the guard stammered. "I mean, I was just—"

"Then why we want adjoining room? To sneak back and forth?"

"You don't," the guard said, feeling utterly bewildered. "I just... was saying—"

"Don't say," the man in glasses said. "Don't say anything. How you say in your language, shut the fuck up?"

The guard nodded, and the man with the eyebrows came forward to the desk for the first time. He leaned over it, raising a hand, and the guard winced, bracing for impact. But the man didn't hit him. He merely knocked his hat from his head. It fell to the ground, and they both looked at it silently until the guard bent down and picked it up.

The two men strode off toward the elevator, and the guard watched them with a growing sense of dread. He didn't realize he'd been holding his breath until they'd disappeared inside the elevator. Then, suddenly, as if emerging from underwater, he gasped deeply. He had the uneasy sensation that he'd just very closely dodged a very dangerous bullet. Something bad was going down, and those men were going to be responsible. If he wasn't mistaken, they'd taken the two rooms either side of the woman from earlier.

He glanced at the clock. Five minutes left on his shift. The morning crew would be showing up any minute.

24

Roth leaned over the brick wall at the side of the parking lot. Six floors below, the street was beginning to come to life. A garbage truck was beeping and crashing as it did its work. A police car had pulled up outside one of the buildings, lights flashing. Behind him on the ground, the three backup drones sat silently, like dogs waiting to be given orders.

He went back to the car and looked at the laptop. A black Mercedes Benz with Russian diplomatic plates was parked outside the diner, hazards flashing, and Roth opened the audio channel to the operator in Langley. "Any movement?"

"Yes, sir. Spector's inside the Mercedes."

Roth let out a little chuckle. "How did that happen?"

"He just walked up and spoke to the driver. Probably gave him an offer he couldn't refuse."

"And what about Grechko? He hasn't come out?"

"Not yet," the operator said.

"And Clarice?" Roth said, clicking her feed on his computer screen.

"Still in the cab."

Roth zoomed out to get a better view of the cab's location and saw she was northbound on Sixth Avenue, passing Radio City Music Hall. "Where are you going?" he muttered to himself. Both the Four Seasons and the Russian Consulate were that way, though he couldn't imagine why she'd be going to either of them. He'd been expecting her to get in the car with Grechko and make her escape—she had a suitcase with her—but that hadn't happened. She was in a cab alone, and Grechko was still in the diner. The consulate didn't make much sense—even the GRU would know that the niceties of diplomatic custom couldn't protect a CIA defector—but if she was going much farther than that, the cab would have taken the FDR already. He watched it make its way along Sixth Avenue, and when it came to 56th Street, sure enough, it turned.

He picked up the phone and called Clem. "Are you watching?"

"She's going back to the hotel."

"Looks like it," Roth said.

"Does that even make sense?"

"Not really," Roth said.

"She had a suitcase. I saw her with it."

"Maybe it was something else."

"I don't think so," Clem said. "A *clever girl* like her, she wouldn't bring a suitcase unless she thought she was going somewhere." There was some bite in Clem's voice as she said the words. Clarice had crossed the threshold. She was on her own now. A traitor.

"She's been disappointed then," Roth said quietly, more to himself than Clem.

Clem heard him, all the same, and said, "Things just aren't going her way."

"You mean the photo."

"First, the photo, which put us on to her handler, and by extension her."

"And now she's been told her trip's been canceled."

"It's almost *too* unlucky," Clem said.

Roth was nodding his head, even though she wasn't there to see him. "Someone set her up," Roth said, "and now I'm beginning to wonder if they're doing the same to us."

"I'd be worried about Lance if I were you," Clem said.

"I don't think he's part of this."

"No," Clem said, "but if someone wanted to pull him in, it almost would have been too easy."

"There was no guarantee we'd send him to follow Grechko."

"Really? Who else could it have been?"

Roth didn't answer. She had a point.

"And how much time was there to get someone to the consulate once the picture was received?"

"It would have been possible to get someone else there."

"Sure," Clem said, in that distinctly British tone that reminded him of a boarding school mistress, "but was that likely?"

"No."

"If someone wanted to target Lance, if they wanted to pull him in and wrap him up in emotional baggage, this is how they'd have had to do it."

"I need to talk to him," Roth said.

"He's not going to pick up now," Clem said. "He's in Grechko's car."

"We've been playing into someone's hand."

"Well," Clem said matter-of-factly, "now we know."

"The problem isn't knowing," Roth said with a sigh, "it's deciding what to do about it."

Clem said nothing, though they both knew what the other was thinking.

"Do we still have a wet team in the city?" Roth said.

"We do," she said, her voice betraying a rare hint of emotion. "Thirty-minute lead time."

"Thirty?"

"Luck's in our favor. They were already deployed in the city and just came back online."

"The Russians won't have factored that into their planning."

"No," Clem said dryly. "I dare say they won't."

"Get them to the hotel. No changeover. No debrief. Pull rank on whoever had them deployed. Just get them there and tell them it could get messy."

"You're sure you want to do that?"

"It's a precaution," Roth said.

"You know how things go with precautions," Clem said. "Once they're in position, they have a tendency to make things happen."

"I know," Roth said sadly. "Find out what room Clarice is checked into and get the team as near to her as possible."

"What sort of firepower should they bring?"

"They should be ready for anything," Roth said, "but they're not to make a move. Tell them to hold well back. Even if they hear gunfire, they're not to do anything unless I say so."

"All right," Clem said. "And what do you want them to do about this third drone? Looks like it's not going to be necessary."

"Keep it on the Mercedes for now," Roth said, "as redundancy."

"All right."

"How far out are we on Keyhole?"

He heard her typing on her computer, then she said, "A few minutes. Which target is the priority?"

Roth thought for a moment, then said, "The hotel."

"You're sure? The hotel's not going anywhere."

"Lance hasn't let me down yet. Let's hope today's not going to be the day he starts."

25

Lance sat in the backseat of the Mercedes and waited, gun in hand, for Grechko to open the door. When he did, the look on his face was difficult to describe. There was surprise there, certainly, but also something more —dismay. Dismay that he hadn't seen this coming, or worse, that he had, or glimpsed it, and hadn't done what he could to prevent it. It was too late now, of course—he was a fox with his foot in a snare now—but a moment earlier, just a split second ago, it could still have been different.

"Good morning, Daniil," Lance said, sitting there in the backseat with his Beretta pointed squarely between Grechko's two beady eyeballs. Grechko took in the scene—Lance, the driver, the time it would take to slam the door shut and make a run for it—and accepted reality. He was enough of a professional not to piss himself because of it.

Lance had seen better men than him do worse in the same situation. "Have a seat," he said.

Grechko hesitated only a moment before climbing in. "Thanks for the warning," he muttered to the driver. "Truly excellent service."

"Don't blame him," Lance said. "It's hardly his fault."

"And whose fault is it?" Grechko said, doing his best to sound calm, to give the impression of still having a semblance of control. He comported himself well enough—sat up straight, adjusted his collar, and even, Lance noted, put on his seat belt. He had a good head on his shoulders.

"Before we get into that," Lance said in Russian, speaking as much for the benefit of the driver as anyone, "let's make one thing clear from the outset. I want no misunderstandings. I kill for a living. Bullets in heads. This is just another day in the office for me."

"Understood," Grechko said gravely.

"And you?" Lance said to the driver.

"*Da*," the man said. "Understood."

"Good, then let's get moving."

"Where to?" the driver said.

It didn't matter to Lance so long as they were on the move, but he had no intention of giving the driver free rein. There was a van belonging to a laundry service in front of them, and he said, "Follow that guy for a while. Nice and slow."

The van started moving, and as the car

followed, Lance kept as close an eye on the driver as on Grechko. "You armed?" he said to the driver.

"Of course," the driver said, nodding toward the glovebox. "It's in there. A Nagant."

"A Nagant?"

"Yes."

"You don't find it hard to get ammunition?"

"I don't go through much."

"You're not planning on going through any today, are you?"

"No," the driver said solemnly. "Not today."

Lance looked at Grechko. "And you?"

"Me what?"

"Are you armed?"

"I'm not," Grechko said, and to his credit, he managed to keep a straight face while he said it.

Lance moved his hand slowly and pulled back the lapel of Grechko's leather jacket, revealing the inner pocket. "Don't make me make a mess of this nice car," he said. Grechko leaned forward reluctantly and let him take the gun, a standard-issue *Yarygina* 9 millimeter, and Lance checked it one-handed to make sure it was loaded, then trained it on the driver. "You see this?" he said, holding it up for him to see in his mirror.

"Da," the driver said gruffly.

"Good," Lance said, then, turning back to Grechko, he said, "You didn't seem as surprised to see me as I thought you would."

Grechko eyed him cautiously, choosing his words. He was still playing the game, poor bastard, still hedging as if there was something left to play for. "The question," he said slowly, "isn't how I looked, but how you knew where to find me. Who told you I'd be there? Who tipped you off about that diner?"

"No one."

"And yet, here you are."

"I followed my orders. They led me there."

"And you always follow orders?"

Lance looked at him, sitting there as calm as a cucumber, or, at least, trying to appear so. He said, "Do you?"

Grechko spread his hands. "I'm a bureaucrat. I follow all orders religiously. You could set your clock by it."

Lance nodded.

"I think it's not so different for you," Grechko continued. "You're a military man, after all."

"I was," Lance said.

"You go where you're told to go."

"What are you trying to get at?" Lance said.

"What I'm trying to *get at*," Grechko said crisply, "is that you and I are in the same boat. We both followed our orders and now, here we both are. The men who sent me to that diner are the reason you were there, too."

Lance thought of the photo Roth had received. What Grechko was saying made sense. It had to have come from the Aquarium. "Maybe you're right," he said.

"We're both here at their bidding," Grechko

said. "We're both dancing to the tune of the same fiddle."

"I wouldn't go that far."

"Everything that happens next, what we say to each other in this car, what I tell you, and what you do to me because of it, has been predicated."

"How so?"

"You tell me."

"What do you mean?"

"You came to that diner because you knew how to find me."

"I followed you."

"From the consulate?"

"Yes."

"Because you knew I'd be there?"

Lance looked at him but said nothing.

"There it is," Grechko said. "Same tune. Same fiddle."

"Same dance," Lance said softly. They were quiet then for a moment. Outside, the traffic was still light, but the first signs of the morning rush were beginning to show. Lance looked out at it and said, "It's not the most straightforward way of getting two men together."

Grechko nodded. There was a solemn look on his face, like he'd already seen this encounter through to its conclusion and knew how it was going to end. He said, "I tell you this just so that you bear it in mind."

"Bear it in mind?" Lance said.

"When you're deciding what to do with me."

"All right."

"So you remember that I'm as much a pawn in all of this as you are."

"Maybe we should just hug it out now," Lance said. "Forget that I just caught you having breakfast with my girlfriend."

"If it's any consolation," Grechko said, "she wasn't very happy to be there."

"I can picture that."

"She didn't eat."

"She never does."

Grechko smiled. "She will when she gets to Moscow."

26

Arsen leaned back languorously, almost too languorously, almost lost his balance, and had to grab the side of the desk to steady himself. He was still in the hotel room, sitting in the room's fancy office chair, his feet on the desk and a lit cigarette in his mouth. He drew from it deeply and exhaled straight up toward the ceiling. On the floor next to him was a porcelain coffee mug, which he tapped the cigarette into periodically.

Two laptops sat open in front of him, each showing a grid of twelve boxes. The boxes were camera feeds—twenty-four in total—with little sine curves beneath showing any sound that was being picked up. The curves were flat for the most part, the fields of view empty and motionless. Twelve of the feeds showed differing angles of Clarice's room. There wasn't an inch of the space that wasn't covered. Two more covered her bathroom. Clarice wasn't home, and the room was dark. The cameras, in their night mode, gave everything a ghostly green tinge. There were two more cameras in each of rooms 3817 and 3821, which were also empty. The rest covered the corridor outside the rooms, the elevator, and the lobby on the ground floor. The cameras in the lobby and elevator weren't Arsen's—they were feeds set up permanently by the GRU with the tacit consent of the hotel. They were higher resolution, higher reliability, and better hidden than the cameras Arsen had set up, but also less likely to be of use.

It was on the lobby feed now that he saw his compatriots, Gabulov and Golubev, marching in from the cold. He watched as they checked in, had their fun with the guard, then hauled their asses and their bags into the elevator. They stood next to each other in the elevator, staring at the door opposite in silence like two strangers.

Then Gabulov said, "Did you fart?"

Golubev looked at him but said nothing. Then he laughed.

In the corridor, they crowded each other as they walked toward their rooms, the two of them seemingly too wide for the space. They were in the country at Arsen's request—he'd worked with them before and knew they were competent, though they certainly relied more on brute force than anything that could be described as *finesse*. They were a package deal. Arsen had only ever seen them work together. They weren't his first choice, they weren't anyone's first choice, but they were preferable to the local assets Kirov and the consulate could have rustled up on short notice.

One thing Arsen didn't enjoy about working with them, something he'd had to spend time practicing, was keeping their names straight. At the Aquarium, everyone confused them. Davidov called them Bert and Ernie after the American puppet characters. It was true that the eyebrows on Gabulov resembled Bert. The analogy ended there, though—Golubev looked more like the Cookie Monster than Ernie, if the Cookie Monster wore glasses like Mahatma Gandhi.

Arsen stubbed out his cigarette and got up from the chair, accidentally knocking over the ashtray as he went. He muttered to himself as he brushed the mess with his foot. He'd only been in the room a few hours but already it looked like squatters had moved in months ago. He stepped over the ash stain, as well as his shoes—which lay in the middle of the floor where he'd kicked them off—and went out to the corridor in his socks. "Gabulov, Golubev," he said. "This way."

They were neither surprised nor pleased to see him, though Arsen thought they could have shown a little gratitude—at his prompting, Davidov had signed off on double pay for the lot of them. They followed him into the room, and the man with the eyebrows—Gabulov—said, "Nice place you've got here."

Technically, the two men were equal in rank,

though Arsen had noticed a tendency in Golubev to defer to Gabulov as if he were the superior. Gabulov, for his part, seemed content to play that role.

They were both eyeing the weaponry Arsen had laid out on the bed, and Gabulov said, "I see you're expecting a complete and utter bloodbath."

"I like to be prepared," Arsen said.

"We were told no heavy weapons."

"Moscow is concerned about optics," Arsen said. "They want this to go nice and tidy. But I don't intend to let this son of a bitch get the jump on us."

"That's not really a risk, is it?"

"Have you read the bio?"

"There are three of us," Golubev said, "and he doesn't know we're coming."

"We don't know what he knows."

"If he knew, he wouldn't come."

"We can't afford to take anything for granted," Arsen said. "What we're doing with this guy, giving him this ultimatum, make no mistake, it's like grabbing a tiger by the tail."

Golubev laughed. "So you're telling us we're authorized to use these?" he said, holding up Arsen's KS-23 special carbine shotgun.

"I'm saying this guy is dangerous," Arsen said. "One of their best. So if you want to take the *Vityaz,* take it. I'm keeping the shotgun."

Gabulov slung his bag onto the bed and undid the zipper. Arsen saw the authorized handguns inside, as well as the drills and other tools they would need to pull off the ambush. "The driver from the consulate brought us out to a storage container in New Jersey when we landed," he said. "That's where we got the drills."

"And lasers?"

"Those too," Gabulov said, "though I don't know what they expect us to do with them. It's not a cat we're playing with."

"He just needs to know he's in trouble," Arsen said. "He needs a reason to listen to what we have to say."

Gabulov picked up the *Vityaz* and said, "I'm on your page, Arsen. I prefer too much firepower to too little. To hell with what Moscow said." He began loading the *Vityaz* into his bag, and he and Golubev each took some flash-bangs.

Golubev said, "Shouldn't I have the shotgun? We're the ones with shooting positions."

"No," Arsen said. "If I have to enter the room, I need to be able to threaten them both at once."

"I thought the girl was doing the talking."

"That's the plan," Arsen said, "but obviously it depends on how cooperative she's planning on being."

"She better be planning on being *very* cooperative," Golubev said, "if she doesn't want her neck wrung."

"I met her this morning," Arsen said.

Gabulov looked up. "And you think she'll be trouble?"

Arsen shrugged. "Let's just say she's willful."

Gabulov nodded. He looked from Arsen to Golubev and said, “We should get going. We’ve got drilling to do.”

“Wait,” Golubev said. He was standing in front of the laptop, and there was movement on one of the feeds. Clarice was in the lobby. “There she is now,” he said. “Our money shot.”

“Honey trap,” Arsen corrected. “And you two should stay. We can surprise her.”

Golubev grinned. “You’re not afraid of facing her alone, are you? I hope she’s not *that* willful.”

“She’ll be more pliant if you two are in the room.”

Golubev shrugged. “Fine by me. If you want me to say hello to your lady friend, I don’t mind at all.”

Arsen felt an unexpected pulse of emotion. “What’s that supposed to mean?”

“What’s what supposed to mean?”

Gabulov, picking up on the tension in Arsen’s voice, said, “He meant nothing. It was a joke.”

Golubev, oblivious, kept on barging forward. “I hear she’s a real piece of ass.”

Arsen gave him a look then that he wouldn’t mistake. For some reason, he was feeling strangely protective of Clarice—a feeling that was frankly ridiculous given what was about to happen. But feelings were what they were. They didn’t need to make sense.

“All I’m saying,” Golubev continued, “is that, if she’s still alive when all this is over, I’d like to give her a good, long—”

Arsen lunged for him, trying to grab him by the throat, but Gabulov intercepted. "Enough, both of you. She'll be here any second."

Arsen took a breath. Golubev was laughing.

"You're a real asshole," Arsen said. "You know that?"

Clarice was in the elevator, standing with her back to the wall and her eyes shut. There was a strained expression on her face. She clearly knew something was wrong. The three men watched her on the high-resolution feed, and a moment of quiet fell over them. It was Golubev who broke it. "All I'm saying," he said, making a little hammering motion with his fist.

"Come on," Gabulov said, "cut it out."

Arsen was tempted to go for his throat again but restrained himself. He watched the screen until the elevator came to a halt, then went to the door. "Be ready," he said, taking hold of the handle. "And watch where you put your ugly mitts," he added. "She's pregnant."

27

Lance was staring intensely at Grechko, and Grechko, in turn, was squirming under that gaze. It wasn't intentional on Lance's part. It wasn't an intimidation tactic. He was just lost in his thoughts, wondering about this man, about him and Clarice, and just how well the two of them knew each other. Had they *been* together? And if so, at whose bidding? Whose initiation? Who'd wanted it more?

He pictured them, her with her sharp fingernails digging into the flabby white flesh of his buttocks, her teeth biting into his neck. He heard her groan on penetration. Had she used all the same tricks on Grechko she'd used on him? Was that all any of it was?

"Here's a question for you," Lance said. "How much of a game are we going to make out of all this?"

Grechko looked startled at the question. "I don't know what you mean."

"You know what I mean," Lance said. "We're having a nice time chatting here and all, but there *is* a gun in your face. You're a hair's breadth from getting your head blown off, and you know it."

"I don't think we're getting on that badly, are we?"

"You recruited my girlfriend."

"It wasn't personal."

"Easy for you to say, Grechko. You're not the one who's been lying next to her while you slept."

Grechko didn't flinch at that. He didn't show anything at all. Lance realized he was staring again and forced himself to smile. Grechko smiled, too, though there was no mirth in it. He had a gun in his face, after all. He was fighting for his life.

"Why don't we skip the small talk and get straight to the meat and potatoes?" Lance said.

"Fine by me," Grechko said, "but you haven't told me what you want to know."

"Come on, Grechko. You're smarter than that."

"I wasn't trying to be smart," Grechko said.

"All of it," Lance said. "I want to know all of it."

"Of course," Grechko said, swallowing.

The car came to a halt, and Lance shifted his attention to the driver. He did so every time they stopped moving, though he didn't think the driver was stupid enough to try anything. The man had to know he wasn't the target. He was on US soil, under diplomatic cover. He had to know no one would want to deal with the mountain of paperwork that would come with his death. All he had to do was stay cool and he'd get through this fine.

They started moving again, and Grechko said, "This would go a lot quicker if you gave me somewhere to start."

"Why don't you tell me how you recruited Clarice? Did you go to her? Did she come to you?"

"We went to her," Grechko said.

"Is that the royal we?"

"*I*," Grechko corrected, clearing his throat. "I went to her."

"Personally?"

He nodded, eyeing the gun before stealing a glance in the driver's direction.

"He's not going to help you," Lance said. "Are you, pal?"

"No," the driver said instantly. "I'm not."

"Wise man," Lance said.

"Such loyalty," Grechko said dryly. "If I make it out of this alive, I'll have to remember to commend you for a medal."

"As long as you don't earn me a bullet," the driver said, "you can commend me for anything you like."

Grechko looked again at the rearview mirror, and Lance said to the driver, "Why don't you turn that thing toward the ceiling."

The driver did so, and Lance turned his attention back to Grechko. He wouldn't be able to trust a word the man said, of course. Roth's first rule of interrogation was to only ever ask questions you already knew the answer to. Like so much of Roth's advice, it had a certain undeniable logic. It was also completely unusable.

"When?" Lance said.

"The recruitment?"

"Yes."

"A few months ago," Grechko said. "Here in New York."

"Before she and I started our thing?"

Grechko nodded, and Lance chewed on that information for a minute, wondering if he'd been the target of the whole thing from the beginning. It would certainly make sense if he was, though there were plenty of other reasons they might want someone like Clarice in their camp.

He eyed Grechko warily. Neither of them had mentioned the envelope. Grechko wouldn't, of course. Not if it was as important as Lance thought it was. "How was she?" he said.

"When I approached?" Grechko said.

"Yes."

"Truthfully?"

"If you don't mind."

"She was... well... no offense..."

"I think we're past that, don't you?"

"Well, she was *easy*, to put it bluntly."

Lance watched the man's face as he spoke, listening carefully to his voice. He still didn't see any sign of deception, though that didn't mean there wasn't any. "You're saying she didn't require much convincing?" he said.

"No, not much."

"Welcomed you in with open arms?"

"In a manner of speaking."

"And that didn't make you suspicious?"

"Everything makes me suspicious," Grechko said. "It's practically the only emotion I feel anymore."

"I know that feeling," Lance said. He waited then, giving Grechko time to say more. When he didn't, Lance said, "What was the objective?"

"The objective? Who wouldn't want a rat in Roth's house?"

"There must have been something specific, though," Lance said. "Something to justify all this risk."

Grechko shrugged. "If there was, it was above my pay grade."

"Now you're just being modest."

"I could hazard some guesses," Grechko said.

"Was I the target?"

"I don't know," Grechko said.

"You don't know?"

"I could see why they would want you. There are a million reasons why the Aquarium would want to get to you, Mr Spector."

"I can't think of a single one," Lance said.

"Now who's being modest?"

The driver was still following the van, which had taken them westbound onto the I-495. They were approaching Queens Boulevard, and traffic was definitely picking up, though they were against it for the most part.

"Where is she now?" Lance said.

"How would I know?"

"Is she being extracted?"

"No. She wanted to be. That's what she was promised."

"But the Kremlin rescinded the offer?"

"They delayed it."

Lance nodded. If that was true, it would probably put her back in their room at the Four Seasons. "All right," he said with a sigh. "I suppose we should take a look at that envelope she handed you."

Grechko's face went pale. It was the kind of visceral reaction that couldn't be faked.

"Didn't know I'd seen that, did you?" Lance said.

"No, I mean, yes, I thought—"

"You look worried about it."

"Worried? Hah! You could say that."

"I am saying that," Lance said pointedly.

"Well," Grechko said, "I'm still trying to figure out whether you're the type of man who'd shoot the messenger."

"You're a lot more than a messenger, my boy."

Grechko nodded slowly. He looked like he wanted to say something else but then changed his mind. He adjusted his position in his seat as if trying, without success, to regain some of the composure he'd had earlier.

"Come on," Lance said. "Let's see it."

"I'll show it to you," Grechko said, "but remember what I said before."

"About us dancing to the same tune?"

"Yes," Grechko said. "Dancing to the same tune. My being a pawn in all of this. I truly was just following orders."

"Aren't we all?" Lance said.

Grechko nodded. "I suppose we are," he said. "So, perhaps you'll think of that before doing anything...." His words trailed off.

"Anything?"

"Anything *rash*," Grechko said.

Lance smiled again and nodded toward the briefcase. "I'll try to remember," he said. "Now come on. Let's go."

Moving as if through molasses, Grechko reached down very reluctantly for the briefcase and brought it up onto his lap.

"Nice and easy, now," Lance said.

Grechko moved painfully slowly, turning the little rotary dials on the combination lock as if the longer it took, the less trouble he'd be in when it opened.

"Hurry," Lance said. "Not exactly Fort Knox, that thing."

"No," Grechko said, "though, to be fair, it was only supposed to be taking a very short trip." He placed his fingers on the two buttons that opened the clasps, but before pressing them, he stopped again and said, "Once I show you this, you're going to find it very difficult to continue this nice, civilized conversation we've been having."

"You're just making me more curious," Lance said, adjusting his grip on the gun.

Grechko nodded, the look on his face one of resignation, like he knew exactly what was going to happen when the lock opened. He breathed in, and Lance unconsciously leaned forward to see inside. The clasps clicked, the lid of the case swung open on its spring-loaded hinges, and then everything went black.

There was a loud bang, and the glass behind Lance's head shattered into a thousand pieces as the car suddenly veered wildly to the right. Lance was blinded by the explosion, deafened by the blast, but his body told him that the car had smashed against the concrete guardrail at the side of the highway. It jolted him forward against the back of the driver's seat, and airbags exploded everywhere. The ones in front deflated instantly, the side curtains remained, and Lance peered frantically into the smoke, coughing, struggling to breathe, trying desperately to get his bearings.

He felt the car swerve again, as if coming off the guardrail and entering a one-hundred-eighty-degree spin. Tires screeched on the tarmac, and Lance and Grechko were flung around the back seat like rag dolls, though Grechko less so for having a seatbelt on.

In the front, the driver wrestled manfully with the steering wheel, trying to pull the car out of its spin. With the glass shattered, the smoke cleared almost instantly, and Lance saw that the car was now facing the wrong direction, looking right back down the highway in the direction it had come.

The passengers, then, all three, stared in horror at the 18-wheeler that was hurtling toward them. It jammed on its brakes, but the wall of steel and glass kept rolling toward them, unstoppable as a freight train. There was nothing they could do but brace for impact. Lance shut his eyes, held his breath, and waited out the seeming eternity of that final split second before impact. When it hit, it was like an ocean wave breaking the hull of a ship.

28

Clarice stepped out of the elevator but stopped short when she saw Arsen in the corridor, standing there in his socks like a college dormmate. "You scared me," she said.

"Sorry."

She shook her head. "My fault. I'm jumpy."

"Meeting didn't go as planned?"

She looked at him curiously. "Not exactly," she said, "but I'm guessing you already knew that."

He said nothing for a moment, then, "You'd better come with me."

He retreated back into his room, and Clarice glanced over her shoulder before following. The second she entered the room, she regretted it. To her left, just inside the bathroom and scarcely three feet from where she stood, was a two-hundred-fifty-pound beast of a man. He was holding a gun and had it pointed at her face.

"Arsen?" she said, forcing her voice to sound more calm than she felt.

"Don't worry, Clarice."

Behind Arsen, sitting on the bed with his back to the headboard, was another man. She looked at him—pretentious round-rimmed glasses—and the guy in the bathroom—two bushy eyebrows like the Frida Kahlo portrait—and said, "Who are these creeps?"

"They're part of the plan."

"Not *my* plan," she said caustically.

"We're the cavalry," the man on the bed said in a heavy accent. "We're here to make sure you don't get your head blown off by the target."

"What target?" she said, looking again at Arsen.

"Let me explain," Arsen said. "Just come in and shut the door."

She remained where she was, the door wide open, trying to decide what course of action to take. When the man in the bathroom cleared his throat, she looked at him, at the gun—she hadn't been trained to get into fights she couldn't win—and shut the door with her foot.

"Good," Arsen said. "Now take your coat off. Have a seat."

"Tell Lurch here to put his gun down first."

Arsen spoke in Russian, and Eyebrows lowered the gun a few inches, though, pointedly, did not put it away completely. Clarice moved forward and Arsen said, "Please, your coat."

He wanted her gun, and she threw the coat onto

the bed in front of him. The guy in the glasses checked the pockets but found nothing.

"Where is it?" Arsen said.

"I don't have it."

They locked eyes for a moment until she realized Eyebrows was right behind her. He tried to take her purse, and she recoiled instinctively, "Tell him to stay the hell away from me."

"Please," Arsen said to both of them, as if this was all just an embarrassing misunderstanding, then held out his hand for the purse and said, "It looks heavy. Let me take it."

"How thoughtful," she said, smiling thinly as she handed him the purse. He passed it to Glasses, who rifled through it and found the Beretta. Arsen then gave Eyebrows a nod, and the man patted her down exceedingly thoroughly, lingering on her thighs, ass, and tits before telling Arsen she was clean.

"Where's the other gun?" Arsen said to her.

"What other gun?"

"Don't play games."

"I gave it to Grechko."

"Really?" Arsen said skeptically.

She didn't answer, and Arsen stared at her for a moment, challenging her to defy him. She remained as blank as a sheet of paper. "Check her room," he said to Eyebrows, then he pulled out the chair at the desk and said again to Clarice, "Please."

"Is that the only word you remember?" Clarice said.

"Take a seat. We have some talking to do."

She remained standing obstinately until Glasses took a step forward, then she sat down and tried to make it look like it had been her own idea. She crossed and recrossed her legs, trying to get comfortable, and looked at the two laptops on the desk. There'd only been one earlier, and they both showed a number of camera feeds. It was clear an operation was being planned, and in the hotel, no less.

That didn't bode well. Not well at all.

"All right," Arsen said warily, like he already knew his job was to tell her things she wasn't going to like hearing. "First off, these men—"

"Animals, more like."

"—are Gabulov and Golubev, sent from Moscow."

"For what purpose?"

"To be friends," Glasses said.

She narrowed her eyes at him. "We're not going to be friends."

"Who knows?" he said, a lascivious smile crossing his face.

"*Protection*," Arsen said, eyeing Glasses like he had a mind to throttle him.

Clarice, for her part, gave him the most withering look she could muster—the one that made men's egos literally melt before her eyes in bars. Then she turned to Arsen. He shifted his weight uncomfortably, and she said, in a tone that matched her gaze, "Protection from *what*?"

"So," Arsen began again, speaking slowly.

"Out with it," she said. "What are you idiots planning?"

"It's Moscow's plan," Glasses said.

Clarice didn't even dignify him with a look. Instead, she looked around the room. It was a pigsty, worse even than when she'd seen it earlier. The cup that was being used as an ashtray was full to overflowing, and there was a conspicuous stain on the carpet by her feet where it seemed to have fallen over. On the bed, two large carryalls sat zipped up, presumably belonging to Thing One and Thing Two. The submachine gun was gone, and she guessed it was in one of the bags. She looked at the laptops and noticed the number 3819 beneath a number of the feeds. She could see Eyebrows conducting his search, making a big mess of everything.

"My room?" she said, chewing her lip nervously.

Arsen nodded.

This was not looking good. She'd known Moscow was up to something—that much was clear from her little breakfast meeting with Grechko—but the threat of it seemed to be getting closer by the second. It looked like there were camera feeds for rooms 3817 and 3821 too, and she said, "You're watching the adjoining rooms?"

Arsen nodded again but said nothing. From his face, she could tell that when he opened his mouth it was going to be very bad.

"I need to speak to Grechko," she said.

He shook his head. "I'm afraid that's not going to happen."

"Why the hell not?"

"Orders."

"Orders? From *you*?"

"From Moscow."

She was about to protest when Eyebrows returned. He gave an almost imperceptible nod to Arsen, which could have meant anything, and Arsen pulled out a phone. As he dialed, he looked up and said to her, "I'm going to connect you to the source."

"The source of what?"

"This is the man you've been working for this whole time. It's the man Grechko works for. And I work for."

He said the words almost sadly, like there was an inevitability to them that he regretted. She watched him go through the GRU's archaic authentication process, tediously entering codes to get through the analog routing mechanisms. When he spoke, it was clear from his voice he was speaking to someone he feared. "It's Arsen," he said. He waited, then said, "Yes sir, they've arrived. The girl, too." He looked at the three of them, then put the phone on speaker. "You're on, sir. Everyone can hear."

Clarice, the goons, even Arsen stared at the phone, breaths held, eyes wide with anticipation. There was no sound, and for a few short seconds,

Clarice thought the call had dropped. From Arsen's face, he thought the same, but then a low, guttural sound came on the line, speaking English in the heavy Russian accent that always brought to Clarice's mind a villain from a bad spy movie. "Clarice Snow?" he said. He sounded like he was speaking through molasses. "Are you there?"

She hesitated, swallowed her nerves, then said, "Who am I speaking to?"

"Well, well, well," the voice said, ignoring her question and sounding eminently satisfied with itself, "if it isn't Clarice Snow, the defector who got knocked up for the Motherland."

She looked at Arsen and the other two, scanning their faces for any change in expression. "I don't know if that's—" she started hesitantly.

"Relax!" the voice interjected. "I'm rooting for you."

"I see," she said dryly.

"I have complete faith you'll bring this one home for us."

"Do you?" she said.

Arsen cleared his throat. "I haven't told her exactly what we're going to do yet," he said, speaking like a schoolboy in the principal's office. "I thought it would be best if—"

"I'd like to speak to Daniil," Clarice said suddenly.

Arsen stopped talking, and there was a long pause while they all stared at the phone, waiting for its judgment. At last, the voice said, "I assume you're referring to Grechko."

"My handler."

"I know who he is."

"He's the only person I've dealt with for this entire thing."

"I understand that," the man said, "and I can see how you might feel more comfortable hearing all this from him."

"I was sitting next to him in a diner not twenty minutes ago," she said, her gaze fixed on the shotgun on the bed, "and I don't think he knew a single thing about all this."

"Well, in any case, he's stopped answering his phone."

Clarice reached for her phone and, in doing so, caused Arsen and Eyebrows to pounce forward like they'd just spotted a rattlesnake.

"Relax!" she said, taking the phone from her pocket. She sent a message to Grechko and waited.

"He's offline, and his driver is too," the voice said. "I'd venture to say they've gone and gotten themselves a little *tied up*."

"Tied up?" Clarice said, the tension in her chest beginning to get tighter. "You think he's in trouble?"

"Oh, I think that would be a *very* safe bet," the man said with a chuckle.

"And that's funny?"

"Everything's funny when looked at from the right perspective," the man said.

"And what perspective is that?"

"Well, this whole thing has been very carefully choreographed. Every detail—from the orgasm that impregnated you all those weeks ago to Roth sending a man to follow Grechko to the diner this morning."

Clarice's mouth felt dry. She tried to swallow but couldn't. "What are you saying?" she croaked.

"What am I saying? I'm saying you're toast, my dear, unless you fall into line with the plan I'm about to outline."

Clarice couldn't breathe. She pulled at her collar and opened a button. "You said Grechko was followed this morning?"

"Yes I did."

"Who by?"

"Who do you think? Your lover boy."

Clarice's blood ran cold. She literally felt the shiver on her spine, as if someone had run a cube of ice down her back. "I… thought—" she stammered, then tried again. "What is this?"

"No need to pretend you're surprised," the voice said.

She put her hand on her chest. She needed someone to open a window, but she knew they were sealed. "I'm not pretending."

"You always knew this was about Spector."

"Yes," she said, her eyes darting furtively around the room as if there might still be some route to escape, "but not now. Not like this. Lance is out of the country." Even as she said the words, she knew they weren't true.

Another chuckle. "Is that what he told you?"

"He was sent by Roth. I was there when he received the call."

"I don't know about that," the voice said, "but I'd be very surprised if Lance Spector wasn't with your friend Grechko right at this very moment."

Clarice felt like she was going to throw up. She rose to her feet and went straight to the window, slapping her hands on the cool glass as though trapped by it. She pressed her forehead against the window, and it was almost possible to see straight down the side of the building to the street all those hundreds of feet below. "This isn't possible," she said quietly.

"Not only possible," the voice said, "but inevitable."

"You gave up Grechko?"

"I gave the Americans a nudge in the right direction."

"But Grechko's your man. Why would you throw him to the wolves like that?"

"Why indeed?" the voice said. "Why would anyone throw perfectly good bait in the water?"

Clarice looked out at the New York skyline. The buildings looked like gravestones. The sun, rising slowly in the east, was a death knell. "If Lance is with Grechko..." she said, her voice quivering, unable to complete the sentence.

"Then he's just now finding out that your womb isn't quite as barren as he was led to believe."

She felt cold. She wiped her brow with the back of her hand, and it was clammy.

"Are you all right?" Arsen said, approaching her. "You're white as a ghost."

She looked at him, but it was suddenly as if he was speaking to her from a great distance. There was a ringing in her ears, and it was getting louder by the second. She could see he was saying something, but she couldn't make out what it was. "He's going to kill me," she said quietly. "He's going to kill all of us." Her eyes darted around the room. She felt her breath coming faster and faster. Then she fell.

Arsen leaped forward and caught her before she hit the ground. He pulled her against his chest and said, "You're all right. I've got you."

She looked at him, his eyes—they were brown and just inches from her face. She looked at the two henchmen. Suddenly, she was glad of whatever protection they were going to afford. When she whispered, all three of them leaned in closer to hear what she was trying to say. "You've signed your own death warrants," she said. "I'm looking at three dead men."

29

At the moment of impact, the car was careening in such an uncontrolled spin that the truck hit it as if in a head-on collision. This second impact was not blunted by airbags, and it was the driver who bore the brunt of it. The front of the car crumpled like paper, and the dashboard crushed his legs. The steering column, breaking free of its housing, jutted forward and impaled him through the chest, its silver steel shaft cutting through the center of his sternum as if sliding through butter. It stopped just inches from Lance's face in the seat behind.

Lance lost his sense of time, everything was a blur, and then suddenly, without seeming to go through the intervening span, the car was completely still. Lance blinked. He took a moment to focus. If he'd lost consciousness, it had only been for an instant. He reached up and touched the smooth bore of the steering shaft before him, feeling the warmth of the driver's blood. Then he registered the gurgling and gasping from the driver.

He knew that sound. The sound of a man dying.

There was smoke in the car—he thought it was smoke—then, as his senses came flooding back to him in an overwhelming rush, like a shot of epinephrine, he realized it was the white talcum from the airbags. The part of his brain that was functioning smelled sulfur—from the airbags, he thought, or the trigger explosive in Grechko's briefcase. It was that blasted thing that had caused the driver to lose control.

He turned to Grechko and instantly recoiled. He'd been unlucky, the poor son of a bitch. That side of the car had scraped along the concrete median, and the steel had been ripped open like a soda can. Part of a serrated edge had sliced Grechko's torso open, gutting him like a fish. He didn't seem to know it had happened, he didn't seem to know anything at all, though he was still drawing breath. Lance reached over and checked the pulse at his neck. "Hey," he said, tapping his face. "Hey, Grechko. Come on. Wake up."

The man's eyes rolled and failed to focus.

The briefcase was on the seat between them, and Lance opened it. The documents inside had been charred by the explosion, and he could see the remains of the device that had caused it. Nothing fancy. A simple booby trap. They'd been commonplace during the Cold War. He made sure there were no other surprises, then looked at the contents—a laptop, a newspaper, the envelope.

A noise came from Grechko, a guttural, hollow sound, like a death rattle, and Lance leaned in to hear what he was saying. "What is it?"

Grechko mouthed the word again. "Benzine."

Lance nodded. Gasoline. He smelled it, too.

Grechko was suddenly awake, struggling at the seatbelt across his chest, oblivious to the wound that was going to kill him in the next few minutes.

"Calm down," Lance said. "You're all right."

"I need to get out."

"I know," Lance said, pretending to help him with the seatbelt. It was still fastened at the buckle, but it had also been sliced through. It didn't matter, in any case. Lance had seen enough wounds to know this one would be fatal.

"Hurry," Grechko gasped.

Beyond the confines of the vehicle, beyond the thin layer of nylon from the airbags that cocooned them, Lance could hear the rising noise of a rescue attempt. There was shouting, the clank of steel hitting steel as someone hammered at something, the roar of the traffic on the other side of the highway.

"Help!" Grechko croaked. "Help!"

"They can't hear you," Lance said, making a show of getting the clasp of the seatbelt open. "Tell me what's in the envelope."

"The envelope?" Grechko said, utterly bewildered.

Lance held it up—it was unsealed—and let the contents slide into his hand. They both looked at it, a blurry black and white photograph, a radar scan —no, an ultrasound. Lance's eyes widened. It was the original, from a hospital, and in the bottom left corner was an identification number, a name, a date, and the seal of the maternal ward at Johns Hopkins in Washington.

There was smoke now, and through stinging eyes, Lance read the information.

The date—a few days prior.

The name—Clarice Snow.

"Fire!" Grechko cried, beginning to struggle frantically in his seat. His face and hands were covered in blood, but he didn't seem to have realized that yet. What he had noticed was the smoke —that and the stench of melting plastic as flames began to lap against the nylon of the airbags. His frenzy grew. "Fire!" he cried frantically. "Fire!"

But Lance hardly heard him. For his part, he was staring at the blurry white smudge at the center of the womb in the picture. In a voice that was scarcely loud enough for Grechko to hear above his own panic, he said, "Is this real?"

Grechko didn't answer, and Lance took hold of him and shook him. "Is this real?" he repeated. "Grechko!"

"What?"

"This ultrasound. Is Clarice pregnant?"

Grechko's mind reeled. His eyes darted and dilated. A few hard slaps on the face brought him enough to his senses that he was able to focus on Lance.

"Is it real?" Lance said again.

"Of course it's real."

The flames were beginning to come through the windshield. They licked at the driver's skin, and the stench of burning flesh and hair turned Lance's stomach. The driver was dead, Lance thought, but then a blood-curdling sound came out of him, a scream of such agony that it focused his mind and Grechko's on one thing—the fire that was inching inexorably toward them. The scream was soul-destroying, pure terror and agony, and it stopped as immediately as it had begun.

Grechko's eyes were fixed on the driver, and Lance had to hit him again. "Grechko? How can it be real?"

"For the love of God, get me out of here," Grechko gasped. "Get me out!"

"Clarice can't get pregnant."

"That was the trick," Grechko cried. "That was the trick, and you swallowed it."

"And Clarice? She *agreed* to this?"

But Grechko was no longer processing information. They could both feel the heat from the flames now, and Lance needed to get out of the car if he wasn't going to die with Grechko. He tried to open the door, but it was stuck. He pulled the nylon sheet away from the shattered window, and light spilled in.

"Don't leave me," Grechko cried. "Please!" His

voice was weaker now, losing hope as his body lost more and more blood. Lance gave him a final look. He seemed to have more of his wits about him. He knew he was going to die. "Don't let me burn," he said, his voice barely audible.

The flames were close enough that Lance was shielding himself from the heat with a part of his jacket. The hair on the driver's head took flame and burned up in an instant. Lance drew his gun and handed it to Grechko. "I'm sorry," he said. "This is all I can do for you."

Grechko took the gun and looked at it as if he'd never seen one. Lance turned away and began scrambling out the broken window. He looked back at Grechko when he was clear. The man was holding the gun in his hands but wasn't pointing it at anything in particular. "She did it willingly," he said.

"What's that?" Lance said.

"Clarice," he said, raising the gun to his temple. His eyes were locked on Lance's, and he said, "She couldn't wait to fuck up your life."

And then bang!

30

Lance didn't want to waste any time at the crash site waiting for police and paramedics. He staggered away from the car as dozens of onlookers stared at him with varying degrees of horror on their faces. A trail of debris and destruction stretched back down the highway—shattered glass, burned rubber, spilled gasoline—culminating with the tractor-trailer and crushed Mercedes that were still locked together in an embrace of tangled and torn steel. The spilled gasoline caught fire, sending a snake of flames back toward the stalled traffic and creating a minor panic as some of the drivers feared the flames might reach them. All four lanes were blocked, and some of the cars had halted so suddenly that they'd been rammed by those behind. A cacophony of honking rose from the backed-up traffic, and Lance eyed the people who'd gotten out of their cars and approached the crash.

They presumably intended on being of assistance in a rescue, would-be heroes with nothing but good intentions, but now that Lance was standing before them, staggering from the wreck with blood and engine grease smeared across his face, they backed away as if from a wild animal.

"It's going to blow," he said to them, getting about twenty feet away from it himself as a few of the most foolhardy continued to inch closer. "Get back," Lance said louder. "I'm not kidding."

"You're not hurt?" one of them said, almost as if it was an accusation, and Lance patted himself down to confirm he was indeed in one piece. The car was totaled, and, looking at it now, it was almost unbelievable he hadn't suffered more injury.

"My lucky day," he said wryly.

Flames were coming from the engine block, reaching into the sky and licking at the front of the semi-tractor. Smoke as black as tar billowed into the sky like a beacon.

"Are there others inside?" a man said. He was wearing a navy business suit and was standing well within the potential blast radius, should there be one.

"I told you to get back," Lance said. The man took a few steps away, and Lance said, "There were two others in the car. They're both dead."

In the distance, the wail of sirens could be heard. They'd be there in minutes. Lance began walking toward the concrete barrier at the far side of the highway.

"Where the hell do you think you're going?" another man said. He had blood on his face and pieces of shattered windshield in his clothing. Lance figured him for the driver of the tractor-trailer. He was dazed but otherwise seemed unhurt.

"I'm sorry," Lance said to him. "When the insurance comes through, take the first offer. The car was owned by the Russian government. You don't want to raise a stink with them."

"What?" the man said, stunned, as if Lance was speaking a foreign language.

Lance didn't say anything else but turned and climbed the concrete barrier at the edge of the highway and looked down to the surface street below. They'd been on a stretch of expressway that was elevated, but it was already sloping back down to street level. The drop was only about ten feet. Lance made the jump and landed slightly awkwardly on his ankle, sending a flash of pain up his leg. The crash had shaken him more than he'd been willing to admit, and he'd pay for it now.

With the barest hint of a limp, he hurried across a potholed street toward the high brick wall of a Costco Wholesale. He followed the back of the building until he was out of sight of the people still watching from the highway. He rounded a corner, crossed a parking lot, hopped a chainlink fence—landing more carefully this time—then crossed a shuttered-up construction site.

When he emerged from the site, hopping the same fence a second time, he was on a residential street with row houses on one side and a fifteen-story apartment block on the other. He followed the street as far as the corner of 99th Street and entered the first store he came across. It was a low-rent convenience store—liquor and pirated DVDs on wire racks, a bearded proprietor in a turban standing behind a protective wire cage. The proprietor watched as if a tiger had just walked into his shop.

"Do you have a restroom?" Lance said to him.

The man was wary, but not so wary that he didn't say, "Restroom is for customers only."

Lance looked at him, protected in his cage. He no doubt had a weapon back there. Certainly a phone. "This isn't a robbery," he said. "There was an accident."

"I think you leave," the man said. "Before I call cops."

Lance didn't have time to negotiate. He didn't have time to consider other options. He drew a gun and, without pointing it at the man, said, "Do you have a phone?"

The man was momentarily speechless. He took in Lance—his demeanor, the blood on his face, the gun—then considered reaching for whatever he kept behind the counter to protect himself.

"I'm on the run," Lance said. "Help me, and I'll be gone in a minute."

The man seemed to consider this for a moment,

then reached for the landline telephone on the counter and slid it toward Lance.

Lance yanked the cord from the wall, rendering it useless, then said, "Cell?"

The man hesitated, and Lance adjusted his hold on his gun as if preparing to use it. A cellphone emerged from the man's pocket, and Lance took it from him. "Now get out from back there. Show me the restroom."

The man directed him to a door at the back of the store, and Lance went inside, keeping the door open. "Stand here, where I can see you." The man obeyed, and Lance washed his hands and face. He said, "I'm going to need a clean shirt."

The man didn't respond but watched wordlessly as Lance continued to wash up.

Lance took off his jacket and shirt and wet his neck and hair. He used paper towel to dry off and said, "You got anything I could have?" He took his wallet and counted out five twenties. "I'm not picky."

The man looked around, bewildered. "A shirt?" he said.

"A shirt," Lance repeated. "A sweater. Anything."

"You like the Mets?"

"No, I don't," Lance said.

The man considered this a moment, then led him to a shelving rack in the corner laden with counterfeit sports merchandise. Lance winced as he put on a blue and orange t-shirt and, over it, a gaudy white varsity jacket with blue and orange trim. There was something slightly off about the NY insignia on the front of the jacket, but Lance couldn't put his finger on what it was.

"How do I look?"

The man hesitated, then, in a voice that didn't even convince himself, said, "Not bad."

Lance took a look at himself in a mirror, transferred his belongings and both guns from his old jacket to the new one, then put on a plain black ball cap that was also on the rack. He handed the man back his phone and the cash he'd counted out. "Don't call anyone."

"No, sir," the man said.

31

Clarice was in a daze. She wanted to get out of the chair. They were in her room now, Arsen's two goons having taken positions she knew were intended to intimidate—Glasses standing behind so that she couldn't see him unless she turned around, Eyebrows in front, towering above her like one of those Stalinist skyscrapers built in the fifties. It had been in one of those, she thought now wryly, that she'd sometimes imagined herself living after this whole thing played out. How stupid she'd been, how naïve, to think the Kremlin would honor a deal made with the likes of her.

"I think I'm going to throw up," she said.

Glasses put a meaty hand on her shoulder, almost as if in comfort, though it also served to remind her how close he was if she tried anything.

"You need to calm down," Arsen was saying. He'd established himself on the corner of the bed, facing her with his legs spread apart like he thought he might have something to impress her with. It was all she could do not to raise her foot and stomp him in the nuts.

But she didn't. She didn't do anything. She just sat there, her mind racing, fuming.

"Calm down?" she said, sounding to her own ear almost disturbingly calm, her voice as flat and dead as a slab of marble. "*Calm down*? It would have been better if you'd shot me in the head rather than this—"

She never finished the sentence. She stopped short. Blinked. Arsen had just slapped her across the face. It took her a moment to register the sharp flash of pain. Her eyes watered. "I dare you to do that a—".

He did it again, harder than the first time, then said, "We don't have time to fuck around. You wanted to defect? You wanted to play with the boys on the top floor? This is what it feels like."

She shut her eyes and swallowed her rage. "If you're pinning your hopes on the baby," she said, "on my being pregnant, it's not going to work. It won't stop him."

Arsen raised an eyebrow. "You knew," he said, his voice colder than it had been before, "that he was the target of this operation."

"Not like this," she said.

"You need to trust us. Moscow has a method to this madness, a reason for doing what it's doing. It has trained professionals—"

"Smacking him over the head with information, that's the method. Socking him one. Hardly the plan of the century, and he's not going to respond the way they think."

"And you're an expert?"

"I've had this man inside me," she said, her anger palpable now. "I know him a damn sight better than any Moscow shrink does."

"Listen, Clarice," Arsen said, "I'm going to make this very simple for you. Either you do as you're told, or you, the baby, and Spector all perish here today. That's not a threat. It's a fact. You have no bargaining power, no leverage. He'll be surrounded. Ambushed. So have a think, if you must, but I suggest you pull yourself together and follow this through to the end."

She made to stand, but Glasses had his hand on her in an instant, forcing her back into the seat. It was pointless to struggle. His hand felt like it was made of lead.

"Don't make him hit you," Arsen said. "It will hurt a damn sight more than mine, I can tell you."

Clarice stared at him, imagining all the ways she would kill him if she ever got the chance, then said, "I know how this ends."

"No, you don't."

"You want me to give him the ultimatum."

"We want you to tell him the price for your life."

"To kill Roth?"

"Yes."

"No," Clarice said.

"What no?"

"He won't do it."

"It's a choice between one life and three."

"He'll never accept. He's loyal to Roth to a fault."

"No one's that loyal."

"He is."

"His own life? The life of his unborn child? The life of the woman he loves?"

"He doesn't love me."

"You don't know that."

"*Please,*" she said.

Arsen looked at her a moment, regarded her, what she was saying, and said, "Look, with the confusion he'll be in, you, the pregnancy, danger, and just seconds to make up his mind, there's no way he tells us to pull the trigger. There's no way he lets you die."

Clarice shook her head. "You should have waited until you had me in Moscow. You should have approached him then. Like I agreed with Grechko."

"You really think he'd choose Roth over you?"

"He'll choose duty."

"His own child? His own unborn child?"

She was still shaking her head. "It won't matter. Nothing you say will matter."

"He's not a monster," Arsen said. "He bleeds red."

"You don't know this man. He's a rod of iron. He won't bend."

"I know human nature," Arsen said, rising to his

feet, "and I know iron. It bends just fine under the right pressure."

Clarice felt a tightness in her chest. She'd never felt it before. At first, she thought it was a heart attack, then realized it was panic. She couldn't breathe, couldn't catch her breath. The plan was doomed. She felt it in her bones. "I need to get out of here," she gasped, but Arsen, ignoring her distress, was leaning forward and already undoing the buttons of her blouse.

32

Lance hurried from the convenience store back toward Queens Boulevard. There were no cabs in sight, and when two police cruisers sped by him, sirens blazing, he decided to hop on a westbound express bus just to get off the street. He boarded and quickly found he had no way of paying the fare. They didn't accept bills. "You need a MetroCard next time," the driver said, letting him on nevertheless.

"Yes, sir," Lance said, finding a seat.

As the bus pulled away from the curb, two more police cruisers sped by, and Lance instinctively turned away from the window. It was a useless gesture, they wouldn't be looking for him like that yet, but he was feeling uncharacteristically anxious. His heart was pounding. He needed to calm his nerves. He took a breath, stretched out his leg, and checked his ankle. Sprained, he thought. He looked out the window again and tried to clear his mind.

Clarice. Pregnant. So simple. So impossible.

He took a breath and tried to identify the emotion coursing through his veins. He'd been trained not to be distracted by them, but this was going to be an exception.

Was it true, he wondered. Was she really pregnant? And if so, was the baby even his?

In the depths of his being, somewhere beyond the reaches of his training and his thought habits and his day-to-day discipline, this was a complete and utter crisis, a code red, a vortex of emotion and confusion and all the things he'd put in a box years ago. It was mayday, mayday, mayday. And through it all was a single, cutting thought—if he didn't get to her, Roth was going to kill her.

As the bus crossed the East River on the Queensboro Bridge, he looked out at the spiderweb of steel trusses and scaffolding that held up the enormous structure. He knew he needed to check in with Roth, he needed to report back and take fresh orders, but Grechko's words kept playing over in his mind, distracting him, making him second-guess his next move. "We're both dancing to the tune of the same fiddle." He pictured Grechko's face the moment before he'd shot himself. He'd been onto something. He was right. Someone was playing their fiddle, and the tune was Russian.

What exactly they wanted, and how far they were willing to go in order to get it, remained to be seen, but one thing was certain—the fog of war was beginning to lift.

Certain things were becoming clear to him. Which meant it wasn't such a leap to assume they'd be getting clear to Roth, too. And Clarice.

She must have foreseen this, he thought. She must have known that by getting pregnant, she was allowing herself to become the leverage—her and the baby. She'd made herself a human poker chip. There was no doubt in Lance's mind that the Kremlin's next play would be to put a knife to her throat.

What could she possibly have hoped to gain from it? He couldn't see her angle. If her dream was to end up in a Moscow penthouse painting her nails and sipping Chardonnay—which, from what he knew of her, it very possibly was—there were a million easier ways of getting there. This scheme, this *plan*, if it could even be called a plan, was suicide. Between the forces she'd betrayed in Langley, of which Roth was only one, and those in the Kremlin, her chances of walking away from this were very slim.

He shook his head. Just because he couldn't see it didn't mean it wasn't there. He couldn't fall into the trap of underestimating her. She'd gotten this far, after all. She'd certainly gotten the better of him in more ways than one.

He pulled out his cell and looked at the screen. It had been smashed in the crash but seemed operational otherwise. He thought about calling Clarice, telling her she'd made a mistake, that she was in danger from both sides and needed to cut and run, but he knew she wouldn't believe him.

She'd think he was setting a trap. In any case, it was probably too late for her to run. If she was at the hotel, and he was actually beginning to hope that she wasn't, then her best chance of survival now was to still be there when he arrived. That way, they could cut a deal with Moscow. Between the Aquarium and Langley, you had to have one of them on your side. No one survived them both.

As his mind raced through the angles, he knew Roth would be thinking all the same things. The old man didn't know everything—Lance prayed he didn't know about the baby—but he knew enough. He'd have guessed the basic play by now.

Clarice was the leverage.

Lance was the target.

And Lance was an assassin.

If you knew those three things, you didn't have to be Albert Einstein to figure out the rest. An assassin needed a target. There were a few big fish in Washington, but Levi Roth was certainly one of them, especially in this game. And he would be almost debilitatingly aware of that fact.

He would want Clarice dead. No debrief. No due process. No examination and cross-examination. A bullet in her skull as soon as possible, and if Lance was an obstacle, then he would have to be swept aside. What was it Roth had said earlier? Take her down like the dog she is? That might have been something Lance could have swallowed, but then he'd seen the ultrasound. That was it. That was the play. The whole bag.

Lance dialed Roth's number and suddenly felt as if he was calling a mortal enemy.

"Lance," Roth said, "where are you?"

"Straight to the chase," Lance said, trying to sound as natural as possible. "No, how are you? Are you okay? I thought you'd be hurt?"

"I'm going to assume from the fact you're calling that you're still on two feet."

"Only barely," Lance said, trying to push from his mind the thought that this man was going to order him to kill his own child. Even if he didn't know it, that's what he was going to do. That's what he represented. "I'm on a bus back toward you."

"What about the envelope?"

Lance wanted to say that the envelope had been nothing, that it had been burned up in the crash, but he needed to be careful. Roth would already be watching for the slightest sign he'd been compromised. That's what sleeping with the enemy got you. To say the envelope had been lost would be too convenient. He had to give him something. He said, "I can't make head nor tails of it."

"Coded?"

"Not coded, exactly. Pages from a phone book."

"A phone book?"

"The Yellow Pages, I think. There must be some hidden meaning in them, but I don't see it."

"We'll get Clem on it. Send her photos of the pages. Hold on to the originals."

"Of course," Lance said, wondering where on earth he was going to get his hands on a phonebook on such short notice. They still existed, as far as he knew. He'd worry about it later.

"And what of Grechko?" Roth said.

Lance was still choosing his words carefully. It was a tall order, but he was still hoping Roth would keep him in the loop. He was unlikely to get the kill order, but he might be able to at least confirm Clarice had gone back to the hotel. "Grechko tried to get clever," he said.

"Meaning?"

"Weren't you watching?"

"Drones lost you on the Long Island Expressway."

"There was a crash."

"I thought that might have been you. Clem's accessed the police feed already. The car hasn't been identified, but I'm seeing two casualties."

"Grechko and the driver," Lance said.

"Unfortunate," Roth said. "It would have been nice to speak to them. Get them into an interrogation room."

"Sure," Lance said cagily, trying to detect any hint Roth was doubting him.

"*Very* unfortunate."

"Like I said, he tried to get clever. There was a trap in his briefcase. It startled the driver."

"A trap?"

"A flash-bang."

"Haven't seen one of those in a while."

"Am I detecting a note of skepticism?" Lance said. It wasn't his imagination. He knew what Roth was thinking. He'd have been thinking the same thing in his position. He was thinking Lance had something to hide.

"Of course not," Roth lied.

"You're wondering if I lost my temper. If I caused the crash."

"*Did* you?"

"What do you think?"

"I think this guy's been running your girlfriend right under your nose. That's got to sting. Then someone in Moscow went out of their way to make sure you knew about it."

"Make sure *we* knew about it."

"Then here you are, miraculously crossing the finish line with not so much as a scratch on you."

"Oh, we're a long way from the finish line, Levi."

"All right," Roth said, speaking deliberately. "Let me ask you this. Did Grechko say something that got under your skin?"

Lance pictured Grechko, scarcely thirty minutes earlier, telling him that Clarice had been an *easy* recruit. That she'd played along willingly. That she'd relished the thought of screwing up his life. He found it easier to believe than he'd have liked. "He tried to," he said. "He said Clarice was an easy recruit. That she went willingly."

There was no value in denying that much. He wasn't giving Roth anything he didn't already have. There was no way Roth hadn't pieced together that Lance was the target. What other reason could anyone in Moscow have to gun so hard for Clarice?

He was a killer. A killer with access to all the people that the Aquarium's top floor wanted dead, including Levi Roth.

That's what Roth was thinking. It had to be. What Lance needed now was to ensure he didn't put any more fuel on the fire. That and, most of all, make sure he didn't find out, didn't get even the slightest inkling, that Clarice was pregnant. If Roth found that out, it would be game over for Clarice, for the baby, and likely for Lance, too.

"What else did he say?" Roth said.

"He said she'd relished the chance to fuck up my shit."

"To fuck up your shit?"

"If you'll pardon my French."

"And how was she going to do that?"

"I don't know."

"And did *Grechko* know?" Roth said patronizingly.

"No," Lance said. "Above his pay grade, he claimed."

"*Well*," Roth said, keeping up his exaggerated tone, "if he *said* it was above his pay grade, we might as well pack up now and all go home—"

"He said the op was top floor," Lance said, knowing that was already the assumption. "I figured that had to be true."

"Did he say who on the top floor is running it?"

"We didn't get that far, but if this goes all the way up, then the ultimate target's got to be you, Levi."

"There are a *few* other targets they might be eyeing up."

"You know you're the only juice worth the squeeze," Lance said, playing to his ego.

"That's a bit generous."

"You're the only person in Washington that means anything to them."

Roth was quiet for a moment, then he said, "And *you're* an assassin."

This was it. Lance had one roll of the dice. If he played this right, he might still be the one sent for the final dice roll. "Then, I'm afraid to say it's not looking too good for you, is it, boss?"

"That's very funny."

Lance paused, only for a second, only to create the right amount of tension, then said, "Unless they're going to ask me to honeytrap you."

Roth laughed out loud, tension dissipating as Lance had intended. It was preposterous. The whole thing. That was what he wanted Roth thinking.

"Now you're just getting my hopes up," Roth said.

"What I don't get is how no one thought to put me on the honeytrap circuit sooner."

"There's a thought."

"That should have been our play this whole time."

Roth laughed a little more, and as the laughter subsided, quickly to be replaced by a graver tone, he said, "Was Grechko surprised to see you?"

Through the window, Lance could see that the bus was trying to get onto Second Avenue. Roadworks and traffic were making the maneuver difficult, and the cars behind were beginning to get impatient.

"No, he wasn't surprised to see me," Lance said. "He wasn't surprised at all."

"Hmm," Roth said, troubled. "He'd guessed something was up."

The bus made it through the intersection, pointed in a southward direction, and Lance rose to his feet to let the driver know he wanted off. "The whole thing smells funky," he said, then, as the bus approached 57th Street, he said to the driver, "This is me, chief."

"Where are you?" Roth said.

Lance got off the bus and pretended not to have heard the question. "I take it Clarice didn't run," he said.

"What makes you say that?"

"You'd have mentioned it."

"Right," Roth said. "No. She went...." His words trailed off, and he went silent. Then he said, "I think it's time you came in, Lance. You've had enough excitement for one day."

"I'm just getting warmed up."

"I know you want to be the one to bring her in," Roth said.

"You don't want her *brought in*."

"No. And I don't want her alone in a room with you either," Roth said. His use of the word *room* suggested to Lance that she had indeed gone to the hotel. "There's too much that could go wrong."

"Go wrong. There's nothing she could say that would cause me to lose my direction, Levi. *Nothing*."

"You don't know that. You don't know what she was going to say. You don't know what the Russians planned to use."

"They have nothing," Lance said. "I tell you now, Levi, I wouldn't switch sides on account of her. You know I wouldn't."

"I don't know what I know," Levi said.

"Are you seriously suggesting—"

"I'm suggesting nothing. I'm just saying that someone, presumably someone very intelligent on the top floor of the Aquarium, has taken an awful lot of pains to get you and Clarice Snow in a room together under very specific circumstances. What game they're playing, what exactly they're hoping to achieve by it, I don't know. But I do know a trap when I see one."

"Someone's got to stop her."

"Not your concern."

"If not me, then who?"

"Not your concern, Lance."

"You've got another team."

"You don't need to worry about that."

"But I *am* worried, Levi."

"If you go in there, she's going to make you an offer you can't refuse. I know it. I may not have figured out what it is, but I know that much.

They're going to tell you something. Say something. They're going to get you doubting yourself. Doubting me. Questioning things you thought you knew. I know how these things play out, Lance. They wouldn't be moving in for the kill if they didn't smell blood. This girl, she's got something on you. If you really don't know what it is, that only terrifies me more. They're going to get to you, and once they do, you'll be fucking unstoppable."

"I know, Levi, but—"

"No but."

"I've got to go in, Levi."

"You know what it is," Roth said. "You know what they've got on you."

"I'm sorry, Levi. I'm going in."

"Don't do it, Lance!"

33

"Damn it," Roth cried into the phone. The line had gone dead. He tried calling Lance back immediately but got nothing. He settled for pulling up the terminal on his laptop screen and tracing the number. While the trace was running, he knocked on the screen separating himself from the driver. "Change of plan, Harry. Spanner in the works."

They'd been idling on 59th Street outside the Essex House Hotel, biding their time until one of the hotel's valets moved them along. Roth was staring out the window at the leafless trees. The park looked singularly barren.

"We're not going back to the hotel?" Harry said.

Roth shook his head. "I think I'm going to have to disappear for a while. Can you arrange the jet? Nearest airport to here, but if we have to drive back to DC, so be it."

Harry nodded, and Roth tapped out a quick message to Lance.

It's a trap. If you see Clarice, kill her on sight. That's an order.

He wondered what Lance would do. If he was given a stark choice—Clarice or him, for instance—which would he pick? Was he in love with her? Was it as simple as that? No, he thought. Not that. But something.

He dialed Clem's number.

"Roth?" she said almost immediately. "What is it?"

"We have a problem."

"Why would I expect you to say anything else?"

"Lance is *en route* to the hotel," Roth said. He was looking at the ping of Lance's location on his screen. "Looks like he's on foot. Approaching from the east. Five minutes tops."

"How does he know where to go?"

"I don't know."

"Have you considered the possibility they're in contact? That they're in this together? That they have been from the start?"

There was a thought, a whole new kettle of fish that Roth wasn't in a position to unravel. "He's the reason we know she's the rat."

"We'd have known soon enough anyway. He

knew you'd been tipped off. What did it cost him to be the one to tell you?"

"Chicken feed?"

"And now he knows exactly where to find her?"

"He hasn't called her."

"From his cell. There are still pay phones in New York City, difficult as they are to find."

Roth sighed. At this point, it was possible—anything was possible—but it wasn't the priority. "The hotel's the last place he saw her. That's why he's going back. It's logical."

"You're happy with that? It's *potentially* logical? You're just going to let him waltz in?"

"Of course not."

"So I should give the order?"

"The team's in place?"

"Yes. Thirty-eighth floor."

"Adjacent rooms?"

"No. They were taken."

"We couldn't do something about that?"

"They're all occupied under the same name. Both adjacent rooms and the room opposite."

"The same name?"

"Yes."

"Someone's getting sloppy."

"And here's the thing. You want to know the name they're under?"

"The anticipation is killing me."

"Colin Farrell."

"Collin Farrell?"

"Yes."

"I'm sorry. Should that mean something to me?"

"You don't recognize it?"

"One of ours?"

"Good lord, you really need to get out more."

"Who is it?"

"Never mind. It's just a pseudonym."

"The Russians. They have her surrounded on three sides?"

"Yes."

"Do we know how many?"

"From the hotel record, three guests. One per room. All on Irish passports."

"Irish?"

"Yes, but they're charging more vodka to their tabs than whiskey, if you know what I mean."

"Okay, they've got their pick of rooms, but we have the element of surprise."

"As far as we know."

"And we have four men."

"Best of the best."

"Send the order. Strike in three minutes. Shoot to kill."

"Target?"

Roth hesitated just a moment, then said, "Do you have eyes on Lance?"

"He's just coming within range of the drone. A block away, approaching the back entrance of the hotel on 57th Street."

"Patch the feed to me."

"Done."

"To the team, too."

"What can he be thinking? He knows we're in there. And he must know the Russians are waiting, as well."

"He wants to hear them out," Roth said. "He wants to know what they have to say."

"You think they have something bad enough to get him to turn?"

"They must think they're in with a shot. That or he wants to save the girl. He knows that without the help of the Russians, she's done for."

"She's done for either way," Clem said.

"He doesn't know that. He's gambling our team isn't in place. Or he knows something we don't."

"That's a hell of a gamble."

Roth put a thumb in his mouth and began chewing the nail. Not a thing he did often. "What's your game?" he muttered to himself. "What's your game? She's done for either way. Are you really willing to die for this?"

"He's getting to the door," Clem said. "We're losing drone coverage."

"Cameras inside?"

"Hang on." Clem did some typing and managed to pull up a fuzzy, low-res view of the lobby. Having entered through the back, Lance was nowhere to be seen. "We need to give the order," Clem said. "He'll be upstairs in two more minutes."

"Team's on standby?"

"Awaiting target."

"Target," Roth said, suddenly feeling hemmed in by the car. He opened the door and stepped out into the street, sucking in deep breaths of the cold air. "He's no more guilty than the rest of us, Clem."

"There are cameras in the elevators. I'm trying to access them now."

"We all let her into our boudoir."

"Not the way he did, boss."

"Has he sent you anything? Pictures? Pages from a phonebook?"

"No, and he's entering the elevator now. Bank two. Car three." Clem's voice was getting increasingly urgent. "We've got ninety seconds. The team needs to know now who to kill. It's now or never."

"All right," Roth said, or tried to say, but his voice caught in his throat. He coughed into his sleeve to clear it.

"Repeat that," Clem said. "What's the order?"

34

Lance stepped up his pace, breaking into a jog as he approached 57th Street, eyeing the rear of the hotel with a rising sense of dread. Nothing about this was right. He was knowingly walking into a trap. The Russians had orchestrated everything. They'd pulled the strings so that he'd be there, on their territory, on their terms, dancing to their tune. They were calling all the shots. He was breaking the first rule of warfare—never let the enemy choose the field of battle. This was their game, and they were holding all the cards.

He scanned the building, the windows overlooking the street, the vehicles, the people. In the sky, he thought he spied a drone, though it could just as well have been his imagination. In any case, if there was anything he could have done to throw the Russians a curve ball, to catch them off balance, he'd have grasped it like a drowning man grabbing a buoy.

But there was nothing. It crossed his mind that he could call Clarice. Warn her. Tell her to cut and run. There was an underground parking lot. Would she meet him there? She'd put herself between Moscow and Langley, the ultimate rock and hard place. She'd scared Roth, and put her escape plan in the hands of a bunch of Aquarium backstabbers. It was very rare for someone to get out of a situation like that unscathed. She'd understand that, wouldn't she?

He wasn't so sure. She'd made this happen, after all.

And in any case, it was probably too late. The Russians wouldn't allow it. No one in Moscow was rooting for a romantic ending to this story. No, they would all be firmly on the side of tragedy in Moscow. It was the only ending they knew. This thing either ended with them getting what they wanted or with Clarice lying on the floor of her hotel room with a bullet in her head. Lance had seen it play out too many times to hope otherwise. They would win, or they would blow up the chessboard. That was how they played.

Lance forced the doubts from his mind. Roth was the bigger threat at this point, anyway. The CIA hadn't initiated this. They hadn't asked for it. And now, Roth just needed it to be over. There was every chance he was going to be the target of whatever Devil's pact the Kremlin tried to foist on Lance, and that meant he'd be prepared to kill—Clarice, certainly, but Lance too, if necessary—in order to prevent it.

It boiled Lance's blood to play into the Russian's hands, but as far as he could see, they were Clarice's only chance of walking away from this alive. He'd looked at the angles, he'd run the numbers, and there really was no other way out. If the CIA got to her first, she was done for. No doubt about it.

Which meant Lance had to let the Russians win or, at least, make them believe they'd won.

He knew they would let him get to Clarice's room. They'd let him speak to her. They'd gone out of their way to make that happen. It was their message she'd be giving him, and he'd hear her out. He'd act surprised. He'd act angry. But then he'd agree to do whatever it was they wanted. That was the only way he could get her out of the country alive. They'd whisk her off to Moscow as she'd no doubt been promised, and she'd be out of Roth's reach, at least for now. It would buy them time. He could worry about the rest later.

He slowed as he reached the hotel. There was a steel and glass service entrance that was sometimes used by guests, though usually only by staff. A spare-looking corridor of concrete and unpainted cinderblock led to the lobby. He glanced at the two big security cameras fixed to the ceiling of the corridor, but there was nothing he could do about them now. He would have to take this as it came. He pressed forward, ignoring every fiber of his being that was screaming at him to abort the whole thing. This was a mistake. The Russians were waiting for him. They'd lured him there. He was doing exactly what they wanted.

And yet, he pressed on, passing a kitchen and an enormous laundry operation before entering the back of the lobby through a discrete paneled door. Immediately before him was a bank of elevators, four in total, and he joined a group of Japanese businessmen in suits who were standing outside them, waiting. He glanced around the lobby as he waited, trying not to draw attention to his gaudy blue and orange clothing. There were multiple cameras, multiple security guards, multiple everything. *Abort*, his mind screamed, and he ignored it.

An elevator finally arrived, and the businessmen filed in. They seemed put off when Lance joined them. They eyed his outfit skeptically, as if considering whether it warranted some sort of action on their part, but said nothing.

"Thirty-seven," Lance said to the man closest to the buttons.

The man looked at him pointedly but didn't push the button.

"Fine," Lance muttered, taking out his own room key and swiping it over the control. He pushed the button himself, and an awkward silence ensued. The car rose to the twenty-second floor, where the businessmen got out, leaving Lance in the elevator alone. He glanced upward, wondering if the Russians had a camera in there too, wondering if they were watching him at that very moment, and checked his two pistols surreptitiously inside his coat.

He took a breath. The plan, such as it was, could really only have one thing said in its favor. It was simple. Too simple, in fact. He was going to get off one floor below Clarice's room and use the fire escape to access the stairwell. From there, he would climb one flight, where he would almost certainly be locked out of the thirty-eighth floor. That wouldn't delay him for more than a few seconds, but it might force him to make noise. From there, it would be a simple matter of walking into the trap they'd set for him and hoping for the best. It wasn't really a plan at all—it was a sequence of actions that barely made sense—but it was all he had. There was no time for anything else. And if this deal wasn't brokered with Moscow very quickly, it would be too late for Clarice.

He shut his eyes, pictured the lay of the land—the corridor, the ice machine, the twelve rooms on the left, twelve on the right, the window with its sight lines—and told himself against reason that he knew what was coming. There would be a team, a Russian team. Roth's team would be *en route*, still scrambling, but ready to take out everyone when they got there, which would be an hour at the earliest, too late to stop this. Too late to prevent Clarice from disappearing. If everything went according to plan.

Hmm. So many unknowns. Too many. He didn't put his odds at any higher than fifty percent, and even that was being generous.

He looked at the floor indicator above the elevator door, thirty-two, thirty-three, and then, without warning, the elevator began to shudder, jangling violently left and right as if from mechanical failure. The lights went out, leaving it in complete darkness, and then it stopped with a final sudden jolt that almost knocked Lance off his feet.

Fuck!

35

Arsen had just taken a sip of hot coffee and almost sprayed it all over his screen when he saw Lance Spector strolling into the lobby from a back entrance. "Oh, shit," he said, picking up the mic that put him in secure contact with Clarice, Gabulov, and Golubev in their respective rooms. "Look alive, people. Elvis is in the building."

"Oh my God," Clarice gasped.

"Game time, sweet cheeks. Just do it like we rehearsed and you'll be fine." He could see her on his computer screen, naked by the window like a sailor's wife gazing out to sea, and he had to admit, she truly was a work of art. If this all played out the way Davidov and the top floor hoped, she'd make a worthy rival to Helen of Troy, he thought. Because if Lance lived up to his reputation, there would be a war fought over this woman.

She looked up at the camera, and for a second,

he felt as if she were staring right at him. Holding his gaze, she reached up and pulled out her earpiece, stuffing it between the bed and mattress for safekeeping. He could still hear what was said in the room, but without the earpiece, she could no longer hear him.

"She's offline, boys. We're a go."

Gabulov and Golubev were visible on his screen on separate feeds, both in position next to the holes they'd drilled to spy on Clarice's room. There were separate holes for a camera, for viewing unaided, and for shining laser sights. When it came time for shooting, no holes would be needed. The lasers were for dramatic effect more than anything, but Arsen had little doubt they'd get the message across.

"Sight good," Gabulov said.

Golubev echoed him and added, "I still think we should have put her in the lingerie."

The only reason they hadn't was that she'd convinced them Lance wasn't a fan. "He's more of an *au naturel* guy," she'd said. "Trust me."

And they had.

"Eyes on the prize, gentlemen," Arsen said now. "There's no telling which way this guy charges."

"Aye, aye, boss," Gabulov said.

This was the most delicate part of the operation. Lance had been informed of the pregnancy perfectly, in a manner designed to immediately put him at odds with his own command. Coming here would be in breach of a direct order. That already put him part way down the road toward betraying Roth. Toward betraying his country. Toward doing the unthinkable.

But there was still a long way to go. What mattered next was making him complicit in Clarice's escape. That would be an act of treason. The Aquarium was already Clarice's only refuge. This would make it Lance's too.

And the Aquarium had tricks up its sleeve when it came to this type of thing. They'd done it enough times to develop means of tipping the scales in their favor. For instance, if a mark knew what was at stake, if he had even an inkling of what the Aquarium was going to offer him, then, just by showing his face, he'd be implicating himself. His own side would know how close he'd come to switching sides. There was no such thing as window shopping in this game. You didn't get to ask who was the highest bidder for your loyalty. Attending the meeting was the equivalent of accepting tenders, it was the equivalent of asking a whore for her price. Regardless of what came next, just asking the question was a crime in a wife's eyes. It created *prima facie* guilt. And so it was with spy organizations, who were as jealous as any bride. The target would have the option of accepting the Aquarium's offer or suffering the consequences anyway. As they said on the top floor, "If you're in the brothel, you might as well fuck. You're guilty whether you do or not. " It was a simple fact that a surprising number of powerful men only grew wise to when it was already too late.

And it was a trap Lance was falling into now.

"If he wants to bitch and moan," Arsen said, "we'll let him. Even if he gets violent, knocks her about, whatever he wants to do to her is fair game."

"He can knock the living daylights out of her for all I care," Gabulov said. "I know I would if I was him."

"We're after one thing and one thing only," Arsen continued. "We only need him to hear us out, lean our way, leave things open." Once he'd done that, once he'd heard their offer, he could be forced into doing the rest. He'd dance to whatever tune they cared to play. *Kompromat* 101. "If he looks like he's having difficulty making up his mind, I'll give order number one. That's when we turn on the lasers. Not before."

"Right on her belly," Gabulov said.

"If it still doesn't look like he's going to play ball, I'll give order two. Take them both out. No loose ends. Are we clear?"

"Clear," Gabulov said.

"But wait on my word. No itchy fingers. The top floor's been very explicit. They've put too much into this for it to end with a couple of corpses in a hotel room."

"*If* it can be avoided," Golubev said.

"Which *I* decide," Arsen replied. "Clear?"

"Clear, clear," Gabulov said. "Da, da, da."

Arsen watched Lance enter the elevator. "Target

in elevator," he said into the mic. "Bank two. West corridor. Thirty seconds." There was a bunch of Japanese businessmen entering with him, and for a second he wondered if they could be a backup crew from Roth. No, he told himself. The Aquarium had predicted he'd be alone, either without Roth's knowledge, or against Roth's will, and that there was still at least another thirty minutes before Roth could muster a response crew. Arsen had a clock on his screen counting down the minutes. In fifteen minutes, come hell or high water, with or without what they'd come for, they would be out of that hotel and on their way to the extraction point. Fifteen minutes. It wasn't a lot of time to convince a man to change everything he'd dedicated his life for, to give it all up, to betray everything he believed in. Luckily, they had a very big carrot, and a very big stick.

"Locked and loaded," Golubev said. "Can we test our lasers?"

"Fuck off," Arsen said, aware that he was just trying to get a rise out of him. "The last thing we need is to get her all panicked."

"I bet they go right at it," Golubev continued. "Start fucking like rabbits. I bet he pounds her like a jackhammer."

"You're just hoping for a show," Gabulov said.

Arsen turned down their chatter and turned up the level on Clarice's room. The elevator had stopped, and the businessmen were getting off. "Fifteen seconds," he said into the mic. This was it.

He'd be with her in a matter of seconds, and they'd find out if all this effort had been worth it.

And then came the wrinkle. "Fuck," he said into the mic. "Civilian in corridor."

He zoomed the camera in on the man, a pair of unstylish pleated gray slacks and a yuppy Patagonia vest—a terrible combination, in Arsen's opinion, but this was America. The man was headed for the nearer bank of elevators—approached, arrived, then walked right past them. "Fuck," Arsen said again. Something wasn't right. Something definitely wasn't right. "He's passed the elevators."

"Ice?" Gabulov said.

"Get to your doors," Arsen said. "Prepare for trouble."

And then two things happened. First, the camera watching Lance's elevator went completely dark. Second, another man came out of the same room as the first, this time armed, this time running.

There was a moment of stillness in Arsen's mind, a cold, silent clarity, like a winter sky, and then the overwhelming surge of adrenaline. "Oh shit," he gasped, pushing the button to broadcast. "Abort, abort, abort."

He reached for the shotgun on the bed, but by the time he had it, the door of his room was crashing in. He whirled around, the carbine at waist height and completely unaimed, and pulled the trigger. At the same time, a man appeared in the doorway holding a pistol and silencer. He was just in time to catch a spray of Shrapnel-25 buckshot to the face, which pretty much hit everything on that side of the room, shattering the TV, shattering the coffee machine, shattering the laptops.

The man in the vest dropped to his knees and put his hands to his face. There was something in the air, and for a moment, Arsen thought it was snow, but it was down from a spare comforter in the closet.

The man on his knees gasped for breath, stunned, blinded.

"Too fucking slow," Arsen said, preparing for the second man. "Too fucking slow."

And then he heard it. It was a thin sound, like the ting of an empty can hitting the floor. He saw a flash-bang grenade hit the wall and fall on the carpet three feet in front of him.

Everything went white, then everything went black. Everything became deafeningly loud, then utterly silent.

He dropped to a knee on instinct and raised the shotgun toward the door, but it was no good. Shots were fired, the pulse of a silencer compressing the sound. He felt the bullets enter his chest like the stinging of an insect.

Suddenly, he was very tired. The gun in his hands felt heavy as a tree trunk. With all his strength, he kept it raised, kept it vaguely aimed, and pulled the trigger.

The words on his lips as his last breath left him were, "Fuck you."

36

"Abort, abort, abort."

Gabulov was on his feet before Arsen even finished the words. He grabbed the PP-19 *Vityaz* and was at the peephole of his door quick enough to see a shape pass by. It was a man, headed straight for Arsen's room. He drew a silenced pistol and kicked open the door. Arsen was ready with the shotgun and caught the son of a bitch with a pile of shrapnel to the face.

The man staggered backward, dropping his gun and reaching for his eyes as if someone had just flung a pot of boiling water in his face. Gabulov was about to open the door and finish him off when a second shape flashed by the door, followed by the concussive pulse of a flash-bang exploding at close distance. Even through the door, it was disorienting. There was more gunfire, a second blast from the shotgun, but no more. He saw the second man go down, but not before getting off some shots of his own. Game over for Arsen, Gabulov thought. At least he took two of the fuckers down with him.

But how many more were there? And how had they responded so quickly? Where had they come from? Where was Spector?

He touched his mic. "Arsen down. How copy?"

No answer, and in the silence that ensued, the thought flashed through his mind that maybe they didn't know he was there. Could he lay low? Sneak out later? He got his answer sooner than he would have liked when the wall of his room exploded behind him. He swung around wildly, spraying bullets from the *Vityaz* in a desperate arc that encompassed half the room. Feathers flew from the bed, the reinforced glass overlooking the city shattered, and the frigid thirty-eighth-story air flew into the room as if into a depressurized aircraft. He concentrated fire on the basketball-sized hole in the wall until a flash-bang bounced in through it, followed by a second.

Instinctively, Gabulov turned his face to the wall, shut his eyes, and covered his ears. Bang. Bang. Forcing his body to obey, he slung the gun back up to firing position and sprayed more bullets at the wall. Then, pop! A third flash-bang. He hadn't seen it come in, and it caught him like a jab to the throat. He saw nothing. Heard nothing.

It was the simplest thing in the world for the CIA man to reach through the hole in the wall and get off a few silenced shots—one, two, three—catching Gabulov in the shoulder, in the chest, in the second shoulder. Gabulov, acting more on rage than anything, deaf and blind and scarcely aware of the pellets of lead thudding into his flesh, kept his finger on the trigger of the *Vityaz*. His dying act was to send a hundred-eighty-degree constant arc of fire—thirteen rounds a second, fast enough to hew a tree—into the wall connecting his room to Clarice's.

Then the door behind him crashed open, swinging off-kilter on a single hinge, slamming the wall opposite and falling to the ground as the second hinge gave way. Gabulov spun in time to see a CIA man—the same one who'd shot him through the wall or another, he didn't know—who would have been about to administer the kill shot were it not for the jet of blood spurting from his neck. There was a strange look of surprise on his face—it was always that same expression, no man was ever ready for death when it came—and he dropped to his knees, gurgling through a throatful of blood.

Gabulov looked left to see Golubev standing there, gun in hand, a triumphant look on his face. The look instantly disappeared when he saw the three bullet wounds in Gabulov's chest. "You're hit."

"It's nothing. All in the vest." He said the words with conviction, but they both knew they weren't true. Not wholly, at least. Gabulov could feel the blood soaking his chest. It was sticky, like someone had poured orange juice down his shirt, and he was finding it difficult to breathe. "We need to leave," he said. "There'll be more of them coming."

In the corridor, the man who'd kicked open the door was still alive, though barely. He was squirming on the carpet, gasping for breath, trying to stem the blood from his neck like someone trying to stop a leak in a lifeboat with his hands.

"Are you the one who got me?" Gabulov said to him. The man couldn't answer, and Gabulov glanced back into his room. He looked at the line of pockmarks he'd sprayed into the walls, and his gaze settled on the hole on the opposite side. The one he'd been shot through. "They came at me that way," he said.

Golubev went and checked it while Gabulov did the dying man the final kindness of putting a bullet in his skull.

The shot startled Golubev, who was back almost immediately. "There's no one there," he said. "We need to kill the girl."

He left, and Gabulov heard him kicking his way through Clarice's door. He almost pitied the girl now, leaving the earth as naked and alone as she'd entered it. He was under no illusions his fate would be any different. He wasn't walking away from this. Golubev wasn't coming back for him. He was dead weight now. Injured. A liability.

There was a single gunshot from the room next door.

"Golubev?" he called out.

No answer.

And that was when he felt it, or rather didn't feel it, didn't hear it, never knew it existed, as it is so often with the bullet that kills you.

37

Clarice was on the ground, holding her breath, her fingers digging into the carpet as if the tighter she held on, the safer she would be. Thoughts flitted through her mind like flashes of lighting.

Where was Arsen?

Where was Lance?

What had gone wrong?

She heard the gunfire, the explosions, the sound of doors being kicked in, and knew it was only a matter of time before that carnage came for her.

But what could she do? She was alone, unarmed, naked. She never should have let them take her clothes. "It will highlight your vulnerability," Arsen had said. "It would take a special kind of prick to kill a naked woman in your situation."

She had a feeling she was about to meet just such a prick.

There was more gunfire, more fighting. She pressed her body closer to the carpet and listened.

Footsteps in the room next door, Gabulov's room, then an explosion in the corridor followed by more gunfire. She needed to do something, and she needed to do it fast. To wait was to die. Arsen had taken the Beretta, but, as far as she knew, they hadn't found the Glock. She could get it from behind the refrigerator, but she needed the screwdriver from her purse first.

More noise, more violence, a loud crash in Gabulov's room. She rose to her knees as the sound of more gunfire filled the air, Gabulov firing off the *Vityaz* like his life depended on it, which it no doubt did. There was a break in the fire, and she took the chance to dash across the room, snatching her purse as she dove toward the minibar. Bullets began punching through the wall while she was still in midair. She hit the ground hard, but not before an errant bullet smacked her in the gut. It felt like the impact from a punch, knocking the wind out of her so that she was flat on the ground, gasping for breath.

And there was blood.

So much blood.

A critical amount. It was gushing out of her like someone had just punched a hole in a jerry can. She managed to roll onto her back, but as she looked at the growing pool of blood gushing out of her, she realized two things. One, her baby was already dead. Two, she would be joining it very soon. She put her hands on the wound, and they were soaked instantly. They did nothing to stem the flow.

Bang. Bang. Gunfire. Bang.

Flash-bangs, deafeningly loud. They were mounting an assault next door.

And she was dying.

But that didn't mean she had to go down without a fight. At least if she could get to the gun, she could go out with a bang of her own. She pulled open the front panel of the minibar and tried to yank the little refrigerator out of place, but it wouldn't budge. And the effort of it exhausted her. She was growing weaker by the second.

But she was determined. She didn't know who was fighting outside, she didn't know who was coming for her, but the determination grew in her by the second that they weren't going to find her lying down. She wasn't going to go gently into that good night. She couldn't win. Holding the gushing wound in her stomach, she knew she'd already lost. But she could kill the first son of a bitch to come through that door.

Using all her strength, all her determination, she found the screwdriver in her purse and began loosening the screws holding the mahogany panels in place. She removed them and, with a Herculean effort, pulled out the fridge. She reached behind it, and there was the Glock—Arsen's Glock, the smaller of the two—right where she'd left it.

She should have shot him with it the moment

he'd handed it over, she thought now. She should have shot every man she'd set eyes on that day—Grechko, Arsen, his two stooges, even Lance. She'd have been better off in a pit of vipers than in this mix-up. There wasn't a single one of them not prepared to kill her.

And here was the result. Her, bleeding out, miscarrying, dying. With grim determination, she checked the gun, then managed to prop herself up against the bed, her back to it, facing the door. She wanted to face her killer head-on, and as she watched the door, she knew that when it opened, whoever came in would be the last person she ever saw.

It didn't take long.

It was a single, solid kick from someone trained to break open doors. The wood split along the frame, and the second kick opened it. She pointed the gun squarely at what she expected to be Lance's face.

But it wasn't Lance. It was Golubev. Glasses.

He came in with a grimace on his face like he wasn't going to enjoy what was coming any more than she was. It wasn't true, of course. He had a gun in his hand but hadn't counted on her having one. He rushed forward without slowing down to look, as though he could literally smell the blood that was pooling around her and was desperate to taste it.

She pulled the trigger and immediately lost grip of her gun. The bullet caught him square in the solar plexus. He looked at her then like he couldn't believe what she'd just done, like he couldn't believe the effrontery of it. His gun fell to the ground, but he somehow managed to stay on his feet, like a boxer who'd just taken a punch to the face but was still standing.

There was another gunshot then, this time from out in the hall, and they both knew that their own fight no longer mattered. They were all going to be swept up by the same force, the same common enemy. No one would survive. They were two dinosaurs battling in the shadow of the meteor that would end everything. He didn't even bother to turn and face what was coming.

"Sorry," he croaked, then cleared his throat. His voice was surprisingly strong. "This wasn't how it was supposed to play out. Your old boss just got a jump on us, that's all."

It took Clarice all her strength to muster a reply. "I guess it doesn't much matter now anyway."

And it didn't. Not for Golubev. A figure dressed entirely in black appeared in the doorway behind him and shot him point-blank in the back of the head. Blood and gore flew forward, spattering Clarice as she turned away from it in disgust. When she opened her eyes, she saw the CIA man, gun in hand.

"If you're going to do it, do it," she said.

He pointed his gun at her, and she shut her eyes, waiting for the final release that death would bring. But the shot never came. She opened her eyes. "I'm sorry," the man said--his face was masked, but his voice was younger than she'd expected--and as quickly as he'd appeared, he was gone. She noted that it was exactly the same thing Golubev had said when he'd come to kill her a moment earlier.

And neither of them had been able to do the deed. They'd been singularly disappointing in that regard. And Lance? Where was he? What had felt like a lifetime to her had only been a matter of seconds, a minute at most, but where the hell was he? Arsen had said he was in the building. So, what the hell was taking so long? She felt that if she could just keep her eyes open a little bit longer, she'd be alive when he got there.

But she couldn't.

Her vision dimmed, her breathing grew shallow, her heartbeat slowed to the point it was barely beating at all. And there, in that lack of oxygen, in that lack of blood, she shut her eyes and realized something she'd never have thought she would. She felt regret. Regret for what she'd done, for how it had turned out, and for what it meant, not for her, but for the as yet unborn child. Her child. Lance's child. For the first time since all this began, she cared, and she felt a sadness.

The world began to darken, to turn black, to fade to nothing. She saw nothing, she felt nothing, and just as it was all about to disappear, a final glimpse came to her, not of the world as it was, but the world as it might have been. Flitting electrical signals, the final stray firings of dying synapses, or perhaps something more, perhaps something spiritual, who could say? It was a glimpse of a world in which Lance had entered the room, not Golubev or the CIA man, and he was holding Arsen's *Vityaz* submachine gun. He'd come to kill her, was pointing the gun at her, but when he saw her lying there, in that position, naked, bleeding, desperate, something changed inside him. His ice-cold blood began to warm, his frozen heart began to melt, the look on his face, in his eyes, softened, and he lowered the gun.

He looked at her, and his gaze lingered on her belly. And it wasn't just pity that she saw in his eyes, it wasn't just sympathy, it was love. She wanted to get closer to him, to feel the warmth of his breath, the warmth of his skin. And she wanted him to feel it, too.

They'd come to the end of the line, the end of the hard, rocky road they'd traveled together, and this was all that was left. He'd been ordered to hurt her, but he couldn't do it. In the choice between killing her and facing death himself, he'd chosen the latter. She knew it with the certainty that only death can bring, and the knowing of it was enough for her.

It was enough.

Because beneath it all, the intrigue and the lies, the cloaks and daggers, the backstabbing and plotting, there'd really only been one reason she'd done what she'd done. One reason she'd gone down this dark, lonely path. She'd done it to get Lance to do something she knew he wouldn't otherwise. She'd done it to make him go against his nature. She'd done it to get him to notice her. And then, perhaps, in noticing her, as unlikely as it seemed, to love her.

38

If your goal is to confine someone for a short time—five minutes, say, ten tops—what better place than an elevator? It is, after all, essentially a metal box suspended from a wire inside a narrow concrete shaft. The floor is reinforced steel. The walls are smack against concrete. The only way out is the roof, and that takes time. Time Lance didn't have.

The drop ceiling wasn't much of an obstacle. As soon as the elevator stopped, he was pushing out ceiling tiles and pulling himself up through the T-bar, using his phone for light.

The roof of an elevator car needs to be as strong as the floor—it houses the pulley responsible for hoisting the main cable system, placing considerable strain on it—but it doesn't need to be solid sheet. Rather, most designs employ a pair of steel I-beams, crossed at the center, which provide the necessary structural integrity. Unless the elevator is the size of a phone booth, the gaps between the beams are generally large enough for a man to squeeze through. So it was here, although doing so took up more of Lance's precious time.

Once on the roof, things weren't particularly complicated. The first rule was not to fall. The building was 682 feet tall, fifty-two stories, and the elevator shaft ran the full length of it and then some. But there were other less obvious dangers—moving engine parts, unshielded electrical wires, and most visibly, the cable and counterweight cable, both of which, when moving, could tear the flesh off a man as effortlessly as the blade of a chainsaw.

Lance looked around with the flashlight. On three sides, he was surrounded by raw concrete. The fourth side opened to the other three cars that shared the shaft. Lance listened for a moment to see whether they were still running—it appeared they weren't—then put his hands firmly on the first rung of the ladder. The ladder was tricky—slippery steel bars set into a narrow recessed channel in the concrete—but he didn't have far to go. The distance between floors was thirteen feet. He had to climb a fraction of that, scarcely six rungs on the ladder, to get to the door above.

The main danger while doing so was that the cars would come back online. They were a modern Hitachi ultra-high-speed model and accelerated very quickly to a maximum speed of six meters per second. That, combined with the pulleys, the engines, the cables, the flying counterweights—it wouldn't be pretty.

He felt around the base of the doors, the phone in his mouth, searching for the small electric motors that controlled the opening and closing mechanisms. When he found them, he ripped out their wires, then began the painfully slow process of prying open the doors, inch by inch, with his fingers. It took more than a minute to get a five-inch opening, at which point the unmistakable hum of the pulleys powering up, accompanied by a strong gust of air from the bowels of the building, signaled that he was out of time. He reached through the opening and, in a single motion, ripped open the doors and leaped through. He landed on the thirty-fourth-floor carpet just as the elevator flew by like the blade of a guillotine missing its mark.

Then, it was a mad dash to the fire escape and up four flights of stairs, which he bounded up blindly, three steps at a time. At some point, the fire alarm had been triggered, and orange warning lights flashed in the stairwell.

Headlong, he crashed into a man coming the opposite way, the two of them knocking each other over from the force of the impact. They fell a few steps to the landing below, and it was Lance who came to his senses first. He grabbed the man by the throat, hoisted him to his feet, then shoved him over the side of the rail, giving him a front-row view of a fall he would suffer if Lance let go. He was dressed all in black but for his face, and Lance didn't see anything that identified him as being from one side or the other.

"Who do you work for?" he said, releasing his grip on the man's throat just enough for him to answer.

"Come on," the man gasped, speaking English with a New Jersey accent, terrified by the drop below him. "Don't do this."

"Answer me."

"I just go where I'm told. I don't know who sent us."

"Roth?"

The man looked him in the eye, and Lance saw the acquiescence in him, the surrender. "You know I can't say," he said, which was true, and was also answer enough.

"The girl?"

"The girl?" the man gasped.

"Did you kill her?"

The man, a kid really, definitely younger than thirty, looked like he was about to speak but then reached instead for a gun at his waist. Lance smacked it from his hand, and it fell down the gap between stairs, clanking about six floors below where it drifted into the rail.

"That was stupid," Lance said. The man said nothing, and Lance said again, "Did you kill her?"

He still hesitated, and Lance shoved him further out over the rail so that his center of gravity shifted drastically. It was now all Lance could do not to drop him, and the man knew it. "There were three Russians up there," the man said. "Our orders were to take them out, take out the girl, and take out you, too, if you tried to stop us."

"And did you do it?"

"Do it?"

"Is she dead?"

"No," the man said desperately. "I mean, yes. But I—"

"What did you do?"

"Nothing," the man stammered. "I didn't have to. She was already hit."

"Hit?"

"Shot. By the Russians. There was one of them in there when I found her. She'd shot him, but it looked like he'd gotten her first."

Lance loosened his grip on the man's throat and pulled him back to safety.

"He's dead, if that's what you're worried about," the man said. "Everyone up there's dead."

There was more Lance could have gotten from him, but he didn't have the time. He cut him loose and continued up the stairs. The door to the thirty-eighth floor was locked, but he kicked his way through it. The instant he was in the corridor, he knew he was too late. He felt it the way an animal senses it's being watched. He felt it on his skin.

The air was thick with the smell of sulfur and gun smoke. He listened but, apart from the wail of the fire alarm, heard nothing. What he saw was debris, broken doors, and shattered glass. He counted four bodies on the ground. There would be more in the rooms.

Then he heard a noise. In the straitened confines of his mind, it felt like the loudest sound he'd ever heard. He spun so wildly that if someone had been within arm's reach, he'd have knocked them out with the gun. He faced the source of the noise, his finger on the trigger, but saw nothing. No movement. No enemy. No friend. He remained as he was, completely motionless, completely silent, until the noise repeated. It was the ice machine—ice falling into the tray.

He had half a mind to shoot it just for the fright it had given him but moved on, stepping over debris and corpses, gun drawn. There was a body by the door to Clarice's room, one of Roth's, to judge by the earpiece. Lance had used the same equipment himself a thousand times. Looked like he'd taken buckshot to the face.

In the room opposite, he saw monitoring equipment, laptops, and ammunition. That must have been the control center. He pictured some cigarette-smoking, stubble-faced Russian operative sitting in the chair, staring at the screen, watching him and Clarice the night before, hanging on their every word, praying they'd make love so that he'd have something live to jerk off to. If he was the dead man on the floor, so much the better.

He turned to Clarice's room and saw another body. This one was presumably Russian, the Russian who'd fired the final shot. Lance looked at him for much longer than he needed to, as if his unconscious wanted to delay the inevitable. He already knew what he would see when he looked at Clarice. A sixth sense told him that no one in the room was living. He looked at the corpse on the floor—its stubby features, its coarse hair, its smashed glasses. He stepped over it then but still refused to look at Clarice.

Instead, he looked at the room itself. The walls. The bullet holes.

A nice little trap it would have been if everything had gone according to plan. But it hadn't, had it? Roth had beaten the odds. He'd gotten there early. He must have had a team already in motion when he realized he needed it. A lucky break on his part. Sometimes, things really were that simple. You were lucky. You were unlucky.

It was cloudy. It was sunny.

You were alive. You were dead.

Everything about the room felt different now, unfamiliar. It was difficult to believe he'd slept there, that it was the room he'd woken up in just a few hours earlier. There were items he recognized--Clarice's purse, the bottle of perfume she always brought with her when she traveled, her suitcase.

And there *she* was.

He could no longer pretend otherwise.

He looked at her splayed out, her back to the bed, sitting up like one of those cowboys in a movie who'd died defending the fort to the last. She'd been shot in the gut—a final indignity to a pregnant woman—and there was so much blood that it had stained the carpet red for three feet all around her.

"Oh, no," he said, his voice cracking, his heart breaking. "Oh, Clarice."

Her hand was on her belly, on the wound, as if to protect the baby.

"God forgive me," he whispered.

She was naked, utterly vulnerable, defenseless as a lamb. They said children were innocent when they slept. For everyone else, they had to be dead to get that concession. Clarice had earned it now.

Lance stepped forward and pulled the blanket off the bed. His movements were awkward. The blanket got caught on something, and he had to yank it free, almost pulling the mattress off with it. All the emotion that had been building up inside him, like water behind a dam, finally began to break through.

He got on his knees and covered her with the blanket, wrapping her like a child, then he put his arms around her and held her. When he screamed, it was into the blanket.

Guilt.

That was the emotion he felt.

That was the emotion he deserved.

What man could look at this and not feel guilty? It was as if he was looking at every crime ever committed by a man against a woman—that endless litany that went back to Adam himself, to the beginning of creation, and to Lance's childhood. He thought of his mother. His sister.

Clarice wasn't so different. And now she'd joined them. Clarice and the baby.

"I'm sorry," he said softly.

This was his fault. He'd done this. From the moment the whole damned thing started, the only person who could have saved her was him. And he hadn't done it. That was his crime.

And he would take it to his grave.

39

Three days later.

Roth adjusted his position in the leather club chair. It was a gorgeous piece of furniture, imported from London in the 1850s, and even now, he could smell the richness that came from over a century-and-a-half of diligent polishing. The leather had been brought to such a fine burnish that sitting on it now was like sitting on satin. And yet, he couldn't get comfortable. The fire—ordinarily, there was nothing he'd have liked more than sitting by a real log fire—felt oppressive and suffocating.

Someone was approaching, and he rose to his feet, but it was only the butler. He brought Roth his scotch on a silver tray, ice tinkling in the crystal glass.

"Thank you," Roth said, taking it in his hand, feeling foolish for having stood up.

"Very good, sir," the butler said with a slight nod. "Can I bring you anything else?"

"No, no," Roth said. "I'm fine."

The butler scurried off, and Roth was alone again. He sat back down and tried to settle his nerves. The room was magnificent—mahogany paneling, crystal chandeliers, shelves and shelves of leather-bound tomes. He was in the Eisenhower Building, right next to the White House, and it was one of the few palaces ever purposefully built as such in Washington. It came with all the trappings and finery of the French Second Empire and had been used by presidents for over a century to host meetings that absolutely had to remain off the books. It was a place for meetings that had never happened.

"Levi!" a booming baritone sounded from across the room.

He turned to see the president padding toward him like a sea captain crossing his own deck. "Mr President," he said, rising.

"Sit, sit," the president said insistently, pulling a cigar from his breast pocket and biting it at the nib. "Andrew! Scotch."

The butler was nowhere to be seen, but he appeared with the drink nonetheless, as well as a bucket of extra ice and a set of silver tongs. He put them on the table, and when he'd left, the president fixed Roth in his sights.

Roth felt like looking away but forced himself not to.

"You had a bad day," the president said, speaking with characteristic understatement.

Roth looked back at him. For a moment, he was silent, then said, "Mr President, I have a lot of bad days."

"Aye, I suppose you do. That's why we pay you the big bucks."

"I thought," Levi countered, "that you paid me the big bucks for my good days."

The president smiled sanguinely. He leaned back in the chair and began lighting his cigar, puffing great clouds of smoke into the air. Roth took advantage of the silence to compose his thoughts. He knew the president was concerned, and he knew what he was concerned about. His job now was to assuage those concerns.

The president had brought a thin file with him, and he put it down on the table between them. The cover was blank, but Roth knew what it contained--Clem's report, carefully edited by Roth to make the whole debacle look as little like a disaster as possible. "This," the president said, "was a particularly bad day, wouldn't you say?"

"I think that would depend on your perspective."

"It was a big day for me," the president continued. "I'll tell you that much. The General Assembly in full plenary, our proposal going to the floor, and scarcely a mile from where the vote was set to take place, you're shooting up hotel rooms and causing pileups on the Long Island Expressway." The president's voice was deadly serious. "Do you know what that makes people think?"

"None of those events," Roth said, "were attributed to us."

"Damn it, Roth," the president said, the strain audible in his voice, "the vote failed. You know that, don't you? The cornerstone of a whole new foreign policy, DOA. "

"I don't think that can be blamed—"

"The Russians and Chinese are actively approaching the states that switched their votes. They're saying we don't have our house in order. There are reports they're flat-out asking people what kind of security guarantees they'd accept in exchange for realignment."

"Security guarantees from Russia? They're the wolf at the door. They're the reason nations need security agreements."

"People are saying you're running a leaky boat, Levi."

Roth had been on the brink of retort, but his voice suddenly left him. The words hit him from left field, completely deflating him. There'd been no mention of that in his report. This was coming from somewhere else. *Someone* else. "That's hardly a fair characterization—"

"They're saying the water's about to get choppy, Russia's making waves, China's making waves, and Levi Roth's out in a leaky boat with his ass in the wind."

Roth cleared his throat. His heart was pounding. Where had all this talk of leaky boats come from? "Not a very flattering analogy," he said, buying himself time.

"It wasn't meant to be."

"The Chinese are saying leaky boat?"

"Just tell me what's going on," the president said, putting a pudgy finger on the report, "because this reads like a child's bedtime story."

That was generous. Roth was given a lot of leeway in his role as Group Director, and the truth was understood to be a malleable concept where his work was concerned. Even still, there were limits. The president understood that a report could get a little murky. What he would not tolerate was lies to his face. Whatever Roth told him now had to hold water. It had to be, at the very least, *partially* true. "The report is hazy on a few details, I admit," he said.

"No kidding."

"All right," Roth said, speaking very carefully, knowing what he said could come back to haunt him. "Three days ago, a DHL courier dropped off an anonymous package at the federal building on H Street."

"The report said that much," the president said.

"Yes, and it's true. It's also true that it contained a tip-off about a Russian operative who'd just landed in New York."

"This Daniil Grechko fellow?"

"Yes, sir."

"The report mentioned," the president said,

picking it up and glancing at the flimsy two pages, double-spaced, "that you were concerned it was a trap."

"In my world, everything's a trap. Especially a tip-off like this. Something out of the blue."

"But you pursued it anyway?"

"I had no choice. It contained some information that was pretty alarming."

"What information?"

"Information that could only be known if the Group had been infiltrated."

"I see," the president said, leaning back and puffing on the cigar again. "So you do have a rat?"

"I *did*."

"Where's that in the report?"

"The rat's dead," Roth said quickly. "The contagion's been contained."

"You're sure of that?"

"As sure as I can be, and believe me when I say the last thing we need right now is external interference."

"Your enemies would like to see you pilloried before Congress."

"Is that what you'd like?"

The president's face softened. They were allies, these two, even if their jobs at times put them at odds. They'd seen off enough attacks together to know they could trust each other. "Who was it?" the president said.

"The rat?"

"Yes."

"Luckily, no one. Low-level. A handler."

"A woman."

"Yes, sir."

"The woman they found in room 3819."

"Very good, sir."

"So that's what this was all about? Catching a rat in a trap?"

"Which was achieved."

"And all that business in the report about a surveillance op going wrong?"

"It's not a lie. There was surveillance. It went wrong."

"You made it out to sound like more than it was."

"There was a hope we'd find out exactly what the handler was up to. I wanted to know what they were after and who was running her. That was a surveillance op."

"That went wrong."

"Yes, sir. In the event, I had no other choice but to kill her before getting the information. The Russians had surveillance equipment that would have helped, but by the time I got to it, everything had been fried."

"By who?"

"We don't know," Roth lied. His first flat-out lie. He knew Lance had done it. It was the last thing he'd done before disappearing from the hotel, and it was a worry. A big worry.

"Could it have been done remotely?"

"It could have, sir. The Russians have software

that can make that happen." Everyone had software that could make that happen, even ordinary people, but Roth was a firm believer in never interrupting an opponent while he was making a mistake.

"Hmm," the president said. "It was mostly about the girl, then?"

"It was all about her, sir. We needed her neutralized. And that's what we achieved."

"It would have been nice if you could have done so a little more quietly."

"I apologize for that, sir. Time was very tight. My number one priority was to make sure the Russians didn't whisk her out of the country."

"And you have no idea what their ultimate objective was?"

"I could hazard a few guesses," Roth said.

"Please do."

"We observed her making a handover. An envelope. It was lost in the chase, but based on what the handler had access to, it probably pertained to Group operations."

"Which means...."

"I'll need to do some house cleaning."

The president nodded gravely. He knew what that meant. Often, it included spilling blood.

"So you're telling me this thing is contained? Squared away?"

"I believe so, sir. Absolutely."

"No loose ends?"

Roth swallowed, his heart pounding in his chest,

but he couldn't turn back now. He was already in too deep. "No loose ends, sir." It was his second flat-out lie. Lance was missing. That was very much a *loose end.* A trained killer like that, disobeying orders, going off-grid, there were a thousand ways it could blow up in Roth's face. It could even cost him his life. But to say anything else would be to sign Lance's death warrant. People like Lance were not permitted to simply go dark. They didn't get to punch out when they had a bad day. Roth had to choose. Cover for Lance and bear the responsibility, or order his death. He'd made up his mind.

"Nothing you're worried about?" the president said.

"You have my word," Roth said. "We had a scare. We took care of it. If I'd known your big vote was happening the same day—"

"—You'd have done everything exactly the same."

Roth gave the president a thin smile. "What can I say, sir? I am what I am."

"Which is why we hired you."

"Thank you, sir."

The president drained his glass and rose to his feet. He still had the cigar in his mouth. He extended his hand for Roth to shake, then said, "For what it's worth, that fucking vote was going to fail anyway."

Roth nodded. He'd known already, of course. He'd never said as much, but there was no way in hell Russia and China could be contained via the UN. The whole thing was hair-brained. It had been doomed from the moment the president dreamed it up.

The president left the same way he'd come, and Roth breathed a long sigh of relief. He even drained his drink. The conversation had gone better than he'd dared to hope. He thought back on every detail of it as he was escorted back to his car, but didn't think he'd missed anything. He'd just dodged a bullet. Now, all he had to do was figure out a way to bring Lance back into the fold. He'd give him some time to cool off—Roth knew he was angry—but this was nothing they couldn't get over. Clarice was a traitor. Lance was a big boy. He'd understand, given time.

He climbed into the Escalade and put his seat belt on. "Home, Harry."

Harry leaned back to look him in the eye. "Home, sir? You sure about that?" They'd spent the last few days on the move. First to Switzerland, then London, then Cairo before returning home. Harry knew it was an evasion technique, and he knew Lance Spector was the threat.

"I can't live my life on the run," Roth said. "If he's going to come, he's going to come."

"You want me to call for extra security?"

"Wouldn't do any good," Roth said. "And, in any case, it would raise questions."

"I'll stay then. I'll sleep in the car."

"Nonsense," Roth said. "The regular detail will suffice. Just drop me off like normal."

He raised the divider for privacy and waited until they were well clear of the checkpoint on 17th Street, and the White House's security blanket, before placing a call to Clem. "It's done," he said when she answered.

"And?"

"Could have been a lot worse. He knows we had a rat. He knows we took care of it."

"And he's satisfied with that?"

"He doesn't think we helped his vote at the UN."

Clem stifled a laugh. "Right. That's why it failed. *Kumbaya.*"

"He's not holding a grudge, at least."

"And Lance? Does he know anything about his going rogue?"

"Rogue? That's a bit dramatic, don't you think?"

"What would you call it?"

"I don't know. Offline?"

"Offline? You've got a trained assassin on the loose whose girlfriend you just killed. He disobeyed a direct order, and he won't pick up the phone. For all we know, he's hiding in your bedroom closet this very second, waiting for you."

Roth winced. He didn't like the thought of that, though he knew it was a possibility. There was no doubt in his mind Lance had entered the hotel with the intention of saving Clarice. Finding her dead would not have been pleasant. "How about AWOL?" he said.

"How about out in the cold?" Clem said, a nod to one of her favorite novels.

"Out in the cold," Roth said. "I like that."

"Let's just hope he doesn't stay out there too long," Clem said. "In my experience, assassins are like wolves. You can tell yourself you've got one tamed, but sooner or later...."

"I know, I know," Roth said. Then, more quietly, only to himself, he said, "Sooner or later, you're going to get bit."

AUTHOR'S NOTE

First off, I want to thank you for reading my book. As a reader, you might not realize how important a person like you is to a person like me.

I've been a writer for fifty years, and despite the upheavals my industry has faced, the ups and downs, the highs and lows, one thing remains constant.

You.

The reader.

And at the end of each book, I like to take a moment to acknowledge that fact.

To thank you.

Not just on my own behalf, but on behalf of all fiction writers.

Because without you, these books simply would not exist.

You're the reason they're written. Your support is what makes them possible. And your reviews and recommendations are what spreads the word.

So, thanks for that. I really do mean it.

While I have your attention, I'd like to give you a little bit of background into my opinion on the events portrayed in this book.

Writing about politics is not easy, and I hope none of my personal thoughts and opinions managed to find their way into this story. I never intend to raise political points in my writing, and I never intend to take a stand. I'm one of those guys who stays out of politics as much as possible, and I would hate to think that any political ideas raised in my book hampered your ability to enjoy the story or relate to the characters.

Because really, this is your story.

These characters are your characters.

When you read the book, no one knows what the characters look like, what they sound like, or what they truly think and feel, but you. It's your story, written for you, and the experience of it is created by you when you read the words and flip the pages.

I write about people who work for the federal government. The nature of their work brings them up against issues of national security and politics, but apart from that, I truly do try to keep any views I might have to myself. So please, don't let any of my words offend you, and if you spot anything in my writing that you feel is unfair, or biased, or off-color in any way, feel free to let me know.

My email address is below, and if you send a

message, while I might not get back to you immediately, I will receive it, and I will read it.

saulherzog@authorcontact.com

Likewise, if you spot simpler errors, like typos and misspellings, let me know about those too. We writers have a saying:

To err is human. To edit, divine.

And we live by it.

I'm going to talk a little about some of the true facts that this book is based on, but before I do, I'd like to ask for a favor.

I know you're a busy person, I know you just finished this book and you're eager to get on to whatever is in store next, but if you could find it in your heart to leave me a review, I'd be truly humbled.

I'm not a rich man. I'm not a powerful man. There's really nothing I can offer you in return for the kindness.

But what I will say is that it is a kindness.

If you leave me a review, it will help my career. It will help my series to flourish and find new readers. It will make a difference to one guy, one stranger you've never met and likely will never meet, and I'll appreciate that fact.

Now that those formalities are out of the way, let's talk about some of the events in this book.

~

As you will have noticed, this book is set two years before the other books in the series. While the events depicted here were hinted at in the earlier books, this is where the full story of Lance's dark past with Clarice is finally revealed. My hope is that it has made the character of Lance richer for you and more fully realized.

Finally, I'd be remiss if I didn't tell you that Book Nine in the Lance Spector series, *The Station,* is available now.

So grab your copy. I promise, if you enjoyed the first eight, you're only going to be drawn into these characters more deeply!

God bless and happy reading,

Saul Herzog

GRAB BOOK NINE

DON'T MISS WHAT HAPPENS NEXT.

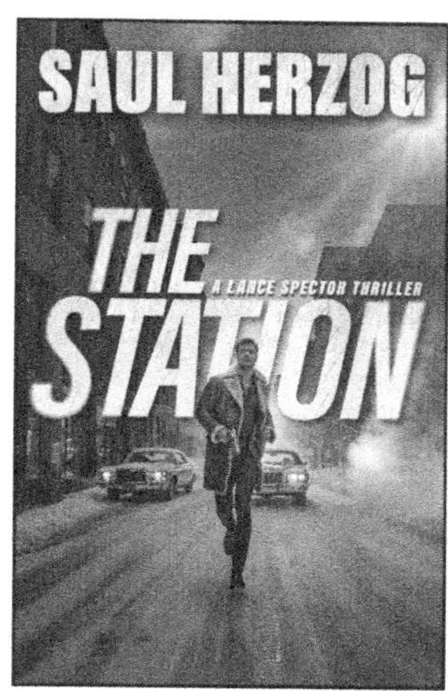

Black Swan, Washington

When a small police station in Washington State calls to say they've found Lance's sister, he has no choice but to go and investigate. What he finds is far more than he bargained for. This stunning climax to the groundbreaking Lance Spector series finally unravels a mystery that stretches from Washington, to the El Paso border region, to the heart of the Kremlin.

Made in the USA
Monee, IL
06 August 2024

63336368R00184